coming home

christine s. feldman

CRIMSON
ROMANCE

F+W Media, Inc.

This edition published by
Crimson Romance
an imprint of F+W Media, Inc.
10151 Carver Road, Suite 200
Blue Ash, Ohio 45242

www.crimsonromance.com

ISBN 10: 1-4405-6593-7
ISBN 13: 978-1-4405-6593-9
eISBN 10: 1-4405-6594-5
eISBN 13: 978-1-4405-6594-6

DEDICATION

To my husband Earl who has taught me what romance really means,

To my very supportive family,

and to Heather and Natalie who taught me the importance of Carpe Diem.

CHAPTER ONE

"Girl, you're lookin' better than a body has a right to."

Callie didn't look up from the notepad she was scribbling in. "I'm all for recycling, Kalvin, but you've used that line one too many times within my earshot for it to work on me."

"Ah, baby, but you're the only one I ever really meant it with."

"Mmm." She kept writing and ignored the teenager's insincere protests of love. He had wandered into the store a few weeks ago, spotted her, and then found an excuse to return almost every afternoon. Points for persistence, she thought.

It was a lazy and very hot afternoon at Vintage Records Your Way, and Callie had little to do behind the counter except write, which was the main reason why she took the job in the first place four months ago. Other than Kalvin, the only other people in the store seemed to be browsing through the merchandise merely as an excuse to avoid the intense heat radiating off the New York City pavement, and that was fine with her. The job was enough to help her make rent, once it was split three ways among Callie and her two roommates. Her boss might be a jerk, but she'd managed to save up enough money to be moving along soon anyway. And the music was good, too. She cocked her head slightly to better hear the strains of Janis Joplin coming over the store sound system and closed her eyes, pencil poised above her paper as she waited for inspiration.

She got more of Kalvin instead.

"Come on, aren't you ever going to go out with me?"

She shook her head.

"Why not?"

"I wouldn't want to ruin the friendship," she said dryly, raising one eyebrow.

"Well, it's not like we're *close* friends . . ."

Giving up on her writing for the moment, she looked at him with fond exasperation. He grinned at her hopefully. The expression was rather adorable on his gawky, young face, and she suspected that he knew it. "Kalvin, why don't you go hit on that girl over there? The one in the pink skirt who's trying to pretend she knows who Blue Oyster Cult is. She's cute, and she's your own age," she added pointedly.

He shrugged and leaned on the counter with his elbows. "Already tried. Struck out."

Callie let out an incredulous laugh. "So I'm your sloppy seconds?"

"Technically," he corrected her with one finger raised in the air, "I think the term 'sloppy seconds' would mean that you were passed on to me after some other guy had you. Which I'm fine with, by the way."

"That's so open-minded of you. Go away now, please, so I can concentrate." She bent over the notebook again.

He strained to see what she was writing. "What are you working on this time? Politics? The environment? Sex and the single girl?"

Suddenly self-conscious, she flipped the notebook over before he could read anything. "It's personal this time, Kalvin."

"Oooh. Like a diary? Going to send it off to *Cosmo* when you're finished?"

But she only waved him off with one hand and scooted her stool back further from the counter so she could write in peace. Grumbling under his breath, Kalvin finally wandered away to give the girl in the pink skirt another try. When Callie was sure he was safely away, she turned her notebook over again and reread what she had already written:

After a while, you start to doubt yourself, to wonder if—on some level—you're looking for him in every man you meet. Looking for his approval. Looking for answers. And it doesn't matter if it's a passing acquaintance or someone who is more of a permanent fixture in your life. You begin to wonder if you're hoping that this time, you'll get it right. Or maybe that this time he'll get it right.

She frowned. It was more wistful than she'd originally intended, which she found vaguely unsettling. This was supposed to be a more clinical piece to submit to a particular journal, a reflection on the effects of absent fathers. They would never accept it this way. Flipping over to a fresh, empty page, she touched her pencil to the paper to try again.

The phone rang then, interrupting her, and she reached absentmindedly for the receiver. "Vintage Records Your Way. What can I do for you?"

"Callie? Oh, good, it's you. This is Tina."

Callie blinked in surprise. It was the more unreliable one of her two roommates. She wasn't very close to either one of them, really. They kept very different hours and rarely crossed paths, and the only other time Tina had called Callie at work was when a pipe had burst in their apartment. A prickle of dread crept down her neck, and she tried to keep the wariness out of her voice. "Tina? What's up?"

"You got a phone call a few minutes ago on the landline, and— look, is there someone else there who can finish your shift for you or something?"

Callie's tension grew. "Manager's in the back. Why?"

"There's been an accident. Your mom's in the hospital."

"What?" she asked sharply, jerking up from the stool and dropping her notebook on the floor. "What kind of accident? Is she all right?"

Hospital. Memories came rushing back at the mere mention of the word. The cop on their doorstep, silhouetted in the night by his patrol car's headlights. Liddy's terror as they rushed into the ER. And Elliot . . .

Eight years ago, and the loss of her brother still felt fresh. It seemed cruel, somehow, that fate would not allow the details of that night to dim from her memory.

"She fell off a ladder or something and broke her leg, I think," Tina said. "I'm not sure of all the details. Guy just said she fell, broke something, and she's in the hospital. Said she should be okay, but asked if you could fly out there."

"That's all you can tell me?"

"Sorry. I'm going on about three hours of sleep here. I wasn't at my sharpest."

Tina worked the night shift at a twenty-four hour bagel shop, which was one reason why she and Callie didn't cross paths much.

"But you're sure he said she was going to be okay, right?"

"Sounded that way, yeah. But he did seem pretty serious, too."

Taking a deep breath, Callie bit back a frustrated response. "Who was it who called?"

There was silence on the other end of the line as her sleep-deprived roommate struggled to remember. "Danny," she said finally. "I think his name was Danny."

An image of him blossomed in her mind, and her pulse quickened. Sandy brown curls, damp as they so often were after a day spent on the river with Elliot. Skin tanned to a warm shade of caramel after a summer in the sun. Strong, lean. And eyes that had captured her then teenage heart the first time she looked into them . . .

She closed her eyes and willed the image away before it could melt her any further.

Danny. How long had it been since she'd heard that name? He must have gotten her phone number from her mother because the last time she'd spoken to him herself was long before she came to New York. And even her mother didn't have her new cell phone number. She felt a twinge of guilt. "Did he leave a number?"

"Sorry. Couldn't find a pencil. Don't worry, though, Cal. Caller ID." Her roommate paused for a moment. Let's see . . . McCutcheon. Is that him?"

"Yes." Amid the turmoil caused by the mention of his name, she felt at least some measure of relief. If Danny said Liddy would be okay, then Liddy would be okay. Then again, Tina's recollection of his exact words couldn't necessarily be counted on to be accurate. And she *had* said he sounded serious. Liddy was not exactly a young woman, and there could be complications with even the smallest of accidents. Callie bent to retrieve her notebook and quickly jotted down the number Tina read her. "I'll be home as soon I can," she said. "You can go back to sleep now."

"Okay." There was a poorly stifled yawn on the other end of the line. "Sorry about your mom."

"Thanks."

Callie dropped the receiver in its place, snatched up her notebook, and grabbed her purse from where it lay behind the counter. Ignoring the curious looks of some of the customers, she pushed open a door marked "Employees Only" and met the startled gaze of her manager, Les. He was a balding skeleton of a man who wore his hair extra long on the sides to make up for the lack of it on top. He was also lazy, a grouch, and a bully.

"What the—who's manning the counter?" he demanded irritably, looking up from the pages of a skin magazine.

"You are," she informed him, looping her purse strap over her shoulder. "I've got a family emergency, and I'm going to need to leave town for a while."

Setting the magazine aside, he folded his long, skinny arms over his chest. "What kind of emergency?"

"My mom had an accident."

"She going to be okay?"

"Probably, but—"

Scowling, he picked up his magazine again. "Then what's the emergency? Forget it. You can't just walk out on such short notice. The schedule's already made for next week. Maybe go the week after."

"I wasn't asking your permission."

His eyes narrowed. "What did you just say to me?"

"I said I'm going to see my mom. I thought a little time off would do it, but a permanent arrangement works just fine, too, you little pissant."

She tossed her copy of the store key at him and walked out as he scrambled to catch it. As she strode toward the front door, she nearly ran down Kalvin.

"What happened?" he asked, wide-eyed.

"A little managerial dispute. Long story short, there's a job opening here if you're interested, kiddo." She gave his arm a quick, affectionate squeeze and let the front door swing shut behind her.

Callie's days there had been numbered anyway. At four months, it was one of the longer jobs she had held, and she was beginning to get that familiar flicker of restlessness that told her it was time to move on. She knew it wouldn't be hard for Les to find a replacement for her. He just didn't like to put down his magazines long enough to conduct any interviews.

Pausing in the sweltering heat, she took a deep breath and dialed the number Tina had given her. It went to voicemail. She wasn't sure if she was relieved or disappointed.

"You've reached Danny McCutcheon's voicemail. You know what to do."

It was a short recording, but it was enough to make her pulse speed up. His voice was casual in the message, warm and mellow. Very different from the last time she'd heard it. She stood there in the middle of the sidewalk with her mouth open, rattled and unable to think of anything to say. Abruptly, she ended the call. Forget it. She'd try again later.

She used the walk home to search online for flights with her cell phone, and by the time she got to her apartment building, she already had a red-eye flight lined up for that evening. There was no boyfriend to say goodbye to and no pets to worry about, not even a potted plant that would need watering. That was the great thing about being a nomad, Callie thought as she threw some clothes into a bag. No strings to tie you down or hold you back.

*

Between packing and dealing with the usual chaos at the airport that happened with a last minute flight, Callie found plenty of excuses to put off trying to reach Danny again. At least for a few hours. But finally, as she settled into a seat near her gate of departure, she fingered the phone in her hand before slowly and reluctantly dialing his number.

Voicemail again. She let out the breath she hadn't realized she was holding and cleared her throat, determined to speak this time.

"Danny? It's Callie. I'm at JFK right now, and my flight leaves in about twenty minutes. I'll have a few layovers, but I should be in Portland by about 10:30 tomorrow morning, coming in from San Francisco." She glanced at her watch. It read 12:02. No wonder she was so tired. "I mean, 10:30 *this* morning, I guess. I'll rent a car or get a cab; I haven't figured that part out yet. Hopefully I'll be at the hospital no later than noon." She paused, feeling that she ought to say something more but struggling to think of the right words. He deserved more than simple pleasantries from her, but she couldn't bring herself to say anything too personal without opening doors best left closed. "Thanks for calling me, Danny. And for being there with Mom. Tell her I'll see her soon."

A woman's voice came on over the intercom to announce that boarding for her flight had begun.

"Gotta go. I'll call you later."

It was a typical red-eye with few people on board, but even with the entire row to herself and the lateness of the hour, Callie remained wide awake and restless. Her mother would be fine, she told herself. Broken bones could heal, and modern medicine would take good care of her. And Danny would see that she was being cared for properly. He had always been good at that, doing his best to fill the hole Elliot's death had left. The two of them had been more like brothers than best friends, and Danny's loyalty ran deep.

Callie leaned back against her headrest and stared out of the window beside her. There was nothing to see but darkness and her own reflection, so she turned away from it and closed her eyes, thinking about home. It would always be the only place she thought of as home, even though she had been in such a hurry to leave it. At eighteen, she had bypassed college and gone to LA for a while—much to her mother's horror—and from there she'd traveled up and down the coast of California, popping back home now and then to reassure her mother that she was still in one piece. They'd argued about it quite a bit: college was too important to skip, life on the road was no life for a girl her age, anything could happen to her . . . Her mother never ceased to come up with a reason why everything Callie wanted to do was a bad idea, but it hadn't stopped Callie from leaving.

Then there was a stretch in Mexico, followed by some time in Louisiana and Georgia. After that she headed north, and the visits and phone calls home had begun to grow fewer and farther between. The conversation was always the same, so it hardly seemed to matter if she called home less often. It only led to more frustration for both of them when she did, anyway.

Liddy had accused her once of leaving just to punish her for her decision to cut everything having to do with Callie's father out of their lives. That was not the reason why Callie had left, at least not consciously, but she knew Liddy didn't believe her. For someone who loved words so much, Callie had a hard time making other people understand why she couldn't bear to stay in one place for too long. Probably because she didn't fully understand it herself. She had met some fascinating people in the process, though, and found plenty of things about which to write.

She opened her eyes again. There was a man she had known in one of those places, one she'd allowed herself to get close to for a time, only to regret it. He had been hurt by the fact that she hadn't wanted him as much as he'd wanted her. She couldn't help it. Somehow, the men she met always fell short. Father issues? Or maybe it was something else. Maybe it was because none of them were Danny.

The last time she had seen Danny had been nearly four years ago. Thanksgiving.

She was in town to visit her mom for the holiday and to break the news that she was headed to the East Coast. Her mother was disappointed. So was Danny.

"So far away?" He had frowned at her. "Why? You hardly see your mom as it is. Family is important, Callie. Don't be so quick to take it for granted."

He disapproved, and she had resented that. So when she left, it was not under the happiest of circumstances, and she thought they both said things they regretted. She wasn't sure how it had escalated but suspected that her part in it had at least something to do with pent-up frustration over the fact that he persisted in seeing her as a kid instead of as a woman. Remembering it now, she smiled humorlessly. For someone who had wanted so badly to be seen as an adult, she behaved rather childishly, and she had spoken to him more harshly than she had intended. Maybe that was why she'd stayed away for so long.

Sighing, she deliberately turned her attention away from Danny and told herself to go to sleep.

But her mind was too busy to allow for much rest. By the time the final leg of her flights landed, Callie was bleary-eyed with exhaustion. She stumbled off the plane, considering her options. A cab would be the more comfortable way to get to the hospital since she could sleep in the back, but it would also cost a small fortune to travel that way over such a distance. A rental car made more sense, she supposed. Throwing her bag over her shoulder once more, she wearily trailed after other passengers through the gate. It had been a few years, but she thought she still remembered the way to the help desks.

"Callie?"

Hearing her name, she blinked in surprise and turned around.

A familiar figure stood off to one side of the crowd, hands tucked casually into the pockets of well-worn jeans as the throng of people jostled past him. In four years, he hadn't changed much, and he looked as much like a lean and tanned man of the outdoors as ever.

Funny how eight years could suddenly disappear and she was right back where she had been as a teenager, at a loss for words at the sight of him.

"Danny?" she managed finally, staring at him. "I—what are you doing here?"

He crossed through the crowd to get to her as easily as if he were crossing water. People just seemed to make way for him, some without even seeming to realize they were doing it. That was always the way with him. He didn't ooze the flashy sort of charm her brother had, the charm that always seemed to win Elliot hordes of female admirers, but Danny McCutcheon had an appeal all his own—one that radiated a quiet, solid sort of confidence.

And Danny had never lacked for female admirers either, much to Callie's teenage chagrin.

He stopped in front of her, his eyes taking her in and impossible for her to read. She felt flustered and had to resist the urge to duck her head as she might have done years ago. It had been a long time since she had trouble looking anybody in the eyes. "Thought you could use a ride," he said.

"Yeah, I could," she said awkwardly, torn between her pride and her sudden desire to throw her arms around him. It was so good to lay eyes on him again that it was almost painful. She hadn't realized how much she'd missed him until he was standing right in front of her. She wondered if he felt anything even remotely like that about her.

They couldn't stand there in the middle of the airport and just stare at each other forever, so finally she gave him a quick, one-armed hug that probably seemed too perfunctory and a little stiff, but it was too late to take it back. "It's good to see you, Danny."

He still smelled like the outdoors, and it still made her lightheaded.

She released him, and his hand brushed against her waist as they separated. "Been a while."

It might have been a rebuke, or it might have been a simple statement of fact. Apparently she had been away long enough to forget how to read him. "How's Mom doing?" she asked, changing the subject.

His face was a mask, expressionless as he studied her. "She's having surgery this morning. Probably be out of it by the time we get there."

"Surgery? For what?"

"She broke her hip. Doctor says if she can avoid infection, she should mend all right, though. She's going to need some looking after."

"I see."

He slipped the bag from her shoulder and put it over his own. "This it?"

"Yeah."

"We're out this way."

Without looking back, Danny led the way through the crowd of people and out to where his beat up old pickup truck sat.

Welcome home, Callie thought with a wistful pang as she followed him out.

*

Danny walked ahead of Callie to allow himself a few moments to absorb the impact of seeing her again. He hadn't expected it to hit him this hard, and he hoped it didn't show on his face.

He hardly recognized her. It wasn't that she looked very different. There were subtle changes, of course, some that he wasn't sure he could even put his finger on, but she still looked like Callie.

But she was different somehow. Older. Harder. Not the same girl he had known. She was a woman now, and she carried herself like one.

She also looked exhausted, Danny thought grimly, as he led the way among the parked cars. There were dark circles under her eyes, and she was much too pale. But then he had always thought that. A little sunshine and fresh air would do her a world of good compared to the smog of New York City. Other than that, though, she was as lean and lithe as ever.

He risked a backwards glance at her over his shoulder. She moved with a confident, sure stride that had not been there before, and when she caught him looking at her, she didn't look away first. He did.

Emotions warred within him. Relief at seeing her safe and sound after years away from home doing God knew what. Bitterness at the easy way she seemed to cut him out of her life despite everything that should have linked them.

But he ought to have hugged her, a small voice inside him insisted. He ought to have held her and told her how good it was to have her back home instead of letting her get away with that aloof little one-armed excuse for a hug. It had been easy enough to do such things when she was his best friend's kid sister, but harder now. This woman walking with him seemed very different from that girl. He wasn't sure he knew her.

She smiled when she saw his truck, and it was a beautiful smile, one that made him suddenly nostalgic for older days when things were simpler between them. "Some things never change, do they?" she asked wryly, running a hand over a dent in the truck's fender, caused years ago in a misadventure with Elliot.

"Nothing wrong with that," he said more shortly than he'd intended.

Her smile faded, and he wanted to kick himself. He didn't want this visit to be a repeat of the last one, full of angry words and hurt feelings. There was a time, after Elliot's death, that he thought they might have been closer to each other than to anyone else. Maybe they would never be able to recapture the easy camaraderie that used to exist between them, but surely they could be civil to each other.

In an effort to be more conciliatory, he opened the passenger's side door for her and handed her the bag after she had settled into the seat. Then he closed the door and walked around to the driver's side, thinking that this might turn out to be a very long ride.

CHAPTER TWO

Callie stole a glance at Danny in the rear-view mirror as he rounded the back of the truck. He wore jeans like few other men could, and he still looked as lean and good as he ever had, but it was the faint frown he wore that caught her attention. Even frowning, his mouth did strange things to her heartbeat.

Judging by his response to her comment about the truck, he still harbored some disapproval of her decision to leave small-town life behind her. Fine, she thought. He could disapprove all he liked. She would make no apologies for choosing to live her life differently than most people did, but she hoped they would be able to put the tension from her last visit behind them. Easier said than done, she supposed.

The door creaked when he opened it up to get in, and then again when he slammed it shut. Most people would have traded the truck in for a newer model by now.

Awkward or not, they were going to have to find a way to talk to each other. "How did it happen?" she asked him. "Mom's accident?"

He turned the key in the ignition, and old as it was, the truck's engine purred like a kitten; Danny McCutcheon took good care of his things. Then he sighed and ran a quick hand through his light brown curls, revealing momentarily the faint line of the scar at his hairline that he had earned the night Elliot had died. "She was trying to put a new display up in the window and fell off her ladder."

"I thought she had someone to help her with that kind of thing," Callie said incredulously. "Debbie Something-or-other."

"She does, but you know your mom. She likes to do the displays herself."

"Yeah, that does sound like Mom." She could be ninety years old and crippled by arthritis, and she would still likely insist on creating the scenes in the storefront window of her little gift shop.

Danny pulled the truck away from the airport and on to the main road, and Callie drew a blank on what to say next. He didn't seem to be in any hurry to talk, so maybe she was the only one who found the silence uncomfortable. She looked out the window and pretended that there was nothing wrong. The city traffic thinned out once they got on the highway, and trees began to pop up beside the road with increasing frequency: pines, firs, and others she couldn't name anymore, if she ever could. Danny knew them all, she was sure.

They were pretty, whatever their names were, and although she enjoyed the New York City skyline, she had to admit that the trees were a pleasant change of scenery.

The air conditioner had long ago stopped working in this truck, and the air in the cab was hot and stuffy. Callie had worn a long-sleeved blouse over a tank top, anticipating the cool air on the plane, but now she was sweating. Rolling down the window, she closed her eyes as a gust of air hit her face, offering some relief from the summer heat. At least here there was no humidity.

She thought she felt him watching her, but when she turned her head to look back at him, his attention appeared to be solely on the road. "Business on the water going well?" she asked, pleased that she finally thought of something to say even if it wasn't exactly brilliant conversation. The rafting business had been both his dream and Elliot's, and she supposed the tourists were out in droves now thanks to the seasonal heat.

"It's a busy time of year for us," he conceded, still not looking at her.

She smothered her growing frustration. "I'll bet." She was a city girl now, but a ride down the river sounded good even to her at the moment. Not that he had invited her. She fanned herself with one hand. "It was good of you to take time away from work to help Mom out. Is your Grandpa minding things for you while you're gone?" she asked, dimly recalling the man who had raised Danny while his parents were . . . well, she didn't actually know where his parents were. Danny had never spoken about them.

It seemed like an innocent enough question to her, but she could have sworn a shadow crossed his face. "No," was all he said.

Callie gave up trying to make conversation. He could talk to her when he was ready. Might as well try to get a little rest before they got to the hospital. Peeling off the blouse she wore over her tank top, she wadded it up into a makeshift pillow against the door and relaxed her head against it. In moments she was asleep.

*

Danny glanced at her. From the deep and even sound of her breathing, he could tell she was sleeping. When she slept, the hardness around her mouth relaxed, and she looked more like the Callie of old. Younger and more innocent. Living on her own terms had toughened her, and he wondered again why she had chosen to leave home in favor of life on the road. When he'd told her he thought it was a poor choice, she had reminded him rather hotly that he was neither her father nor her big brother, and it was not his place to try to tell her what to do. Maybe she was right, and he had to admire the guts it took for her to go out on her own, but the idea of her disappearing into the great wide world had hit him like a ton of bricks. She and Liddy might not be family to him, but except for his grandfather, they were the closest things to it that he had left. He admitted to himself that he had not handled it well at the time, but the fact that it seemed so easy for her to leave wounded him.

He turned his attention back to the road.

She would leave again, once Liddy was back on her feet. It would be wise of him to remember that.

Callie stirred in her sleep and shifted beside him, bringing her leg into contact with his. The touch was very slight, but his grip on the steering wheel faltered for a moment. Her movement had startled him, he told himself, that was all. And yet now his grip on the wheel was unnaturally tight.

But he was not himself. It had been a stressful couple of days, and given the way they had parted last time she was home, it was understandable if things felt awkward between them. Add to that the fact that he was going on precious few hours of sleep, and he was allowed to cut himself some slack.

Of course, she looked exhausted, too. She could use a little slack as well.

He let her sleep until they pulled into the parking lot of the hospital, and then he had no choice but to wake her.

"Callie." Danny said her name softly, so as not to startle her. She moved slightly but didn't wake, so finally he reached out to touch her hand with his own. Her fingers curled around his automatically, and he froze, unwilling to break the moment. It was just because it was good to have his friend back again, surely. His surrogate sister. He worried about her being so far away from home and it was simply good to be able to reassure himself that she was here and safe, if only for a short time.

But the feel of her hand in his now was very different from what he had expected. He had held her hand before, many times, and it had never done this to him. Her skin, so soft and pale against his own tanned and calloused palm, sent a spark of something through him that he didn't recognize. At least, not with her.

Resisting the urge to brush his thumb over her fingers one more time, he withdrew his hand from hers and spoke her name again, louder this time. "Callie. We're here."

Her dark eyes flew open with the confusion of someone who had been sleeping deeply and was unsure of her surroundings. Then they locked onto his, and he saw comprehension dawn.

"We're at the hospital?" she asked, rubbing a crick in her neck and arching her back in a stretch.

His fingers tightened on the steering wheel again, and he looked away from her profile. "Let's go find out if she's awake."

*

Callie had never imagined her mother as frail before, but as she looked down on her sleeping mother's face now, she thought she looked much older and smaller than she remembered. Liddy was only fifty-three, but there were far more lines on her face now than the last time Callie had seen her. Natural aging? Or worry lines? If she couldn't tell, then she had probably been away too long, Callie thought with a pang of guilt.

"The surgery went well. We cleaned the area thoroughly and put some screws in the femur. She'll be on antibiotics for a while, but she should heal just fine."

Callie nodded numbly at the doctor's words, but her gaze remained on her mother.

"When do you think she'll be able to go home?" Danny asked from somewhere behind her, and she felt a surge of gratitude that he was there and able to think clearly enough to ask what should have been an instinctual question for her.

"Not for several more days at least. We'll want to make sure she doesn't develop an infection after the surgery. She'll spend a few more days here, and then we'll move her to a rehab facility for a few more days after that. We're going to give her a walker and have her work with our physical therapist to learn the activity limitations she needs to follow as the hip heals." The doctor gave them a meaningful look. "She's going to need a lot of help for a while. Things that used to be simple will suddenly be a lot harder until she learns to adapt. Don't be surprised if you meet with a little frustration from her now and then."

"We'll take good care of her." Danny held out his hand. "Thank you. We appreciate everything you've done."

The older man smiled and shook it. "Absolutely." Then he turned to Callie. "Don't worry, young lady. I suspect your mother will make a fine recovery."

Callie snapped out of her daze. "Thank you," she said politely, but it was disconcerting to see Liddy like this, she who never got sick with anything worse than the common cold. She was the very definition of an independent woman, and Callie couldn't remember ever having seen anything take the wind out of her sails before.

"Oh, and she just had a dose of pain medication before you arrived, so she'll probably be sleeping for a while." The doctor opened the door to go. "Come back tonight, and she'll be more alert and ready for visitors, I think." The door swung shut behind him.

When he was gone, Callie took a tentative step closer to the bed. She watched her mother's chest rise and fall with shallow breaths beneath the hospital gown and half-expected Liddy's eyes to pop open and the older woman to speak. But she only lay without moving.

Danny's hand touched Callie at the small of her back, reassuring. "She'll be up and complaining about the food before you know it."

"She looks thin. Was she always this thin?" Callie was ashamed that she couldn't seem to remember.

"Hospital beds make everyone look sickly. And the lighting doesn't help, either. Don't pay any attention to that stuff."

"Easier said than done." Reaching out, she took one of her mother's unresponsive hands in her own and squeezed it. "You think she knows we're here?"

"Yeah, I think she does."

Bending down, she whispered into Liddy's ear. "Hey, Mom. It's your prodigal, here. I understand you had yourself a little bit of trouble at work. Quite the drama. What you won't do to drum up a little business, eh?"

There was no twitch of the eyelids, though, and no answering squeeze of the hand. Callie straightened, disappointed but not really surprised.

Danny put an arm around Callie's waist and gently drew her away from the bed. "You heard the doctor. We can come back tonight."

His arm was strong and steady, and she was tempted to lean into it. Not so much because she was worried—she believed the doctor's encouraging words were on the level—but more because the closeness felt good after the awkward greeting at the airport. But once they were out in the hall, he let his arm drop away from her. She moved ahead of him so he wouldn't see the disappointment on her face.

*

Behind her, Danny watched Callie as she briskly navigated her way to the nearest exit. He noticed that she avoided any hallways that might pass near the ER, and he wondered if she felt the same aversion to hospitals that he did now. Liddy's fall yesterday left Danny no other option but to face the cold, antiseptic walls of the emergency room again, and the effect on him had been like a punch to the gut. If it had been anyone else but Liddy, he might not have been able to do it at all.

Standing there in the waiting room, listening to the occasional curt announcement on the intercom whenever a doctor was paged, he had immediately been drawn back to the night Elliot died.

It had happened near the railroad tracks. The other driver, dead drunk, slammed into their driver's side door, and Elliot had taken the brunt of the impact. It all happened so quickly; Danny could really only remember coming to afterwards.

The blood in his eyes. The pain in his head. The eerie angle of the other car's headlights as they lit up the shards of glass that were all that was left of the driver's side window. And the utter stillness of Elliot, slumped over the steering wheel.

It was hard enough to accept it himself, harder still to be the one who'd had to break the news to Liddy and Callie.

Oh, yes, he could understand Callie's haste to get out of this building.

*

They drove to Liddy's house, the same house in which Callie and Elliot had grown up. Callie was quiet most of the way, staring out the window at familiar streets and landmarks. Here and there were a new business or a tract of homes that she did not recognize, all reminders that she had been away long enough for changes to happen.

A knot formed in her stomach that got worse as they got closer to the house. She rubbed the palm of one hand, surprised to feel that it was clammy in spite of the heat of the day. After all, she still had a fondness for this place, even if she did tend to stay away from it. It was the memories, she supposed, and the feelings they invoked. They were better left buried. Less painful that way.

Danny pulled the truck into the driveway, and Callie stared at the house. Two-story, cheerful yellow siding, window boxes brimming with cascading pink petunias. The front lawn had been recently mowed, and a handmade wooden birdfeeder on a pole hosted several guests. Elliot had made that birdfeeder when he was eleven years old.

A sudden pang hit Callie, and she swallowed hard.

Danny noticed. "What's wrong?"

"Nothing." Callie grabbed her bag with one hand and got out of the truck without waiting for him. She wanted to be alone when she stepped inside the house again, and she still had her old key. Taking a deep breath, she opened the front door.

The house was the same on the inside, too. She stood in the open doorway and let her eyes roam over the front room, the staircase, and the pictures on the walls. Dropping her bag on the floor, she stepped into the living room and let her fingers trail over the back of the couch, the end table. How many hours had she spent here hanging out with her friends when she was younger? And with Elliot . . .

She moved on to where a collection of family portraits hung on the wall. There was her mom, much younger and with far more blonde in her hair than the gray that was there now, her arms around her two young children. Elliot's broad grin, highlighted by his braces. Callie's dark pigtails. The pictures traced the children's growth into adolescence under their mother's watchful smile.

There were no pictures of Callie and Elliot's father, though. There had been once, but not after he left, even though Callie could remember begging her mother to put one back up. It was one of many things over which they butted heads.

Leaving the pictures behind, she wandered to the foot of the stairs and looked up. Would her mother have packed up most of her things, much as they did with Elliot's? She had every right to do so, but Callie knew it would hurt if she had. Sliding her hand along the banister, she went up the steps and down the hall to her old room. She opened the door and was relieved to see that other than the absence of a few childhood knickknacks, everything else looked just as she remembered from her last visit here a few years ago.

Had it really been almost four years? She had her reasons for staying away, but she felt ashamed now that it had been so long.

She would sleep in this room tonight.

Elliot's room was further down the hall. With slow steps, she approached it and opened the door. The comforter on the bed was not the one her brother had used. Liddy replaced that one long ago with one that was more neutral and less likely to remind her of her son every time she passed by that room. Callie sat down on it and smoothed out a few wrinkles on its surface.

There was a day, shortly after the funeral, when she'd stood in this room surrounded by her brother's things. Old soccer trophies, t-shirts tossed casually across the bed as if he would be coming back momentarily to fold them, a framed photo of Elliot kayaking on whitewater with his paddle raised up over his head in a gesture of triumph and his face lit up in a grin . . .

Callie closed her eyes and remembered.

Just sixteen years old, she stood there with a large cardboard box at her feet, wondering if she had the strength to do this but knowing it would be far too painful for Liddy to do. Reaching out, she picked up a sweatshirt with trembling fingers.

Someone reached out to take the shirt from her, and she turned to see Danny, his forehead still bandaged from the accident.

He folded up the sweatshirt for her and placed it into the box. "Your mom said you'd be doing this today," he said, not making eye contact. "I thought . . . maybe you might want some help."

A creak of the floor brought Callie back to the present. Looking up, she saw Danny standing in the doorway. Their eyes met, and she knew he was remembering that day, too.

"Still feels like he should be here sometimes," she said.

"Yes, it does."

There were no more wrinkles left on the comforter, but she pretended that there were so that her hands would have something to do. The silence grew heavy, and finally Callie put her hands in her lap and stared at them.

"So, how long will you stay?" he asked her, folding his arms across his chest.

"I don't know. Depends upon how long she needs me."

"What makes you think she didn't need you before?"

Her head shot up. "My mother doesn't need me to live right in the next room for the rest of my life."

His voice was clipped. "There's a big difference between moving out and moving all the way across the country."

Callie pushed herself up off the bed, her temper flaring. This was just about the same place where they left off four years ago. They might as well get it out in the open instead of continuing to tiptoe around it. "And here we go again. Déjà vu. It's not like I'm the first person to ever leave home before, Danny."

"But you went as far away as you could get, didn't you?"

"Just because you're happy in Rockford Falls doesn't mean it's the right place for me."

"Do you even know where the right place for you is? Because it sure seems like you're having a hard time picking a place and settling down."

"Settling down is overrated."

"Ah. Is family overrated, too?"

"You think I don't appreciate family?" she asked angrily. "Just because I moved away?"

"I don't know how you feel about family. You're never here for me to ask. What I do know is that I speak to Liddy a hell of a lot more often than you do. You want to cut me and everybody else from Rockford Falls out of your life? Fine, that's your choice. But what about Liddy? She may not need you to live down the hall, Callie, but she needs to hear your voice once in the while."

That stung, partly because she knew there was some truth to it. "My relationship with my mother is complicated, Danny," Callie said stiffly. "And you don't really have a right to pass judgment on it."

"I think being the one she has to turn to instead of you gives me some right."

She bit back a bitter laugh. "My mother doesn't need me nearly as much as you seem to think."

"Actually, she does." Danny left the doorway to stand directly in front of her. "And I know that because I'm here to see it. She misses you, Callie. Sometimes she feels like she lost two children instead of one."

His words made her stare at him. "Well, some of that was her choice," she said finally.

He frowned. "What do you mean?"

"Ah, so maybe you *don't* know everything after all."

Before he could respond, the cell phone in his shirt pocket rang. Pulling it out and looking at the caller ID, he left the room without another word to take the call. Callie followed him as far as the door. Danny stood at the end of the hall, head bowed and one hand on the back of his neck as if to ease sudden tension there. She felt an unexpected urge to touch him, to rub away the knots that troubled him.

She stifled it.

His voice was too low to hear, and Callie told herself she had no right to eavesdrop anyway, so she went no closer. But curiosity flickered inside her. Judging by his demeanor, the call was a personal one. A friend? Or maybe . . . a woman? The thought bothered her more than it should have.

"You'll have to go back to the hospital without me tonight," he said, turning around as he ended the call and thrusting his phone back into the pocket of his shirt. "There's something I have to take care of."

"What? After all that talk about being there for people who need you? A little hypocritical, aren't you?"

He stiffened, and she knew the words were unfair.

"Sorry," she said grudgingly.

"Give your mom my love," he said curtly, and he brushed past her to go back downstairs.

Callie sighed and leaned her head against the doorframe, her anger dissipating.

That could have gone better.

*

Danny slammed the door of his truck closed and started the engine. He had not meant to say any of that stuff to her, and certainly not right after she had seen her mother lying in the hospital. She was absolutely right when she said it was up to her to decide where and how she lived, he just didn't think she fully understood the impact her choices had on others. Like Liddy. And if he was honest about it, him.

Four years she had gone without once picking up the phone and calling him. He'd tried to call her once, when he thought they'd both had plenty of time to forgive and forget, but her number had been disconnected. It was months later that she finally gave Liddy her new number, and whatever reasons she may have had for waiting so long, he was too bitter to want to hear them.

He glanced at the house.

The truth of it was that it had been a hard pill to swallow, that their friendship had not meant as much to her as it did to him. Her presence in his life had been a godsend for him after losing his best friend and had made the loss somehow bearable. Moments that he might have shared with Elliot or that reminded him of his friend turned into moments shared with Callie instead. Like when the two of them grappled for hours with ways to distract Liddy on Elliot's birthday, or when he first broke ground on the site of his outfitter—

That had been a day he remembered often.

Danny stood on the edge of the building site and stared out at the river that surged by. It was everything he and Elliot had hoped it would be, but the knowledge left him feeling heavy-hearted instead of pleased. It didn't seem right somehow that he should go ahead with things as planned, not when Elliot—

"Knock it off." Callie's stern voice from behind him startled him out of his bleak thoughts. She had come with him to see the builders' progress,

although he suspected her willingness to come had less to do with any interest in rafting and more to do with her memories of her brother.

"Knock what off?" he asked in surprise, turning to look at her.

She frowned at him, the expression somehow coming off as matronly on her teenage face. "The guilt trip."

He turned his gaze back to the water, feeling his throat tighten. "He should be here."

"Yeah, he should." She came up beside him to wrap her fingers around his hand,

and he held them fast. "But that doesn't mean that you shouldn't," she added softly. "You lived, Danny. Make that mean something."

He withdrew his hand from hers long enough to put an arm around her shoulders, and the two of them stood in silence then, staring out at the water . . .

Danny blinked, and the image in his mind disappeared. He thought that since Elliot's death, he and Callie had developed a special kinship, leaning on each other through the grieving process and coming out on the other side of it as two people who each knew a side of the other that no one else did.

But maybe he had only imagined it after all.

He leaned back against the seat, and the cell phone in his shirt pocket bumped against his chest, reminding him of the call earlier. This was not the time for a stroll down memory lane.

Because family was important, and right now *his* family needed him.

*

Callie spent most of the afternoon trying to get over her jet lag. Still on East Coast time, she raided her mother's refrigerator and ate an early dinner by West Coast standards. She half-hoped Danny would call, but a part of her was relieved when he didn't. She didn't want to fight with him again.

Things used to be so much easier between them. She missed that.

She missed him.

Biding her time until she would return to the hospital, Callie sank onto her mother's couch and picked up a photo album from the coffee table. She leafed through it, smiling at some of the pictures, fighting back tears at others. She was not one to cry these days, and hadn't been for a long time. Probably because she protected herself from disappointment a lot better now than when she was a child. If she didn't let herself grow attached to things, she didn't miss them so much when they were gone.

She turned a page in the album and came across a picture that must have been taken shortly before Elliot's death. He was forever young in the picture, forever brimming with promise.

Danny sat beside him in the photo, his seat a large rock somewhere in the wooded outdoors he loved so much. Maybe it was the site the two of them had picked out for their rafting business? It was hard to tell without seeing the building itself that Danny had later built. Well, wherever it was, the camera captured the warmth of his smile perfectly.

She ran her fingers over the picture, thinking regretfully of the heated words they had exchanged earlier. It was a sign that he cared, she supposed, that he wanted to push Callie closer to her mother. She wished they could be closer, too. But Danny didn't really know the reasons why they weren't. Back when they were closer, she had come close to confiding in him once or twice about her mother's bullheadedness regarding Callie's father, and now she wondered if things would be different between them if she had.

For a moment, her hand hovered over the phone. She could call him, tell him that despite appearances to the contrary she was glad to see him. How many times had she thought about calling him in the past few years? Too many to count. But his disapproval of her had stung, and for a long time she had doubted that he would welcome the sound of her voice. She had waited a long time to call, putting it off for fear that she would not like the result. And then one day she woke up feeling as if too much time had passed and she had missed her chance.

She left the phone where it was and called herself a coward.

Her mind was restless, but her body demanded sleep after going so long without any except those few minutes in Danny's truck, so she dragged herself upstairs to her old room and curled up on the bed. Weariness won out over anxiety, and her eyes finally closed.

After a long nap that just barely took the edge off her exhaustion, Callie rummaged through her mother's purse that someone—Danny, most likely—had been thoughtful enough to bring back after Liddy's accident. She pulled out the keys to her mother's compact little hatchback, and in the dwindling light of dusk, she drove herself back to the hospital.

She stared at the building for a long moment from inside the car. Get over it, she told herself flatly. She couldn't avoid hospitals for the rest of her life just because of what happened to Elliot. But her grip on the door handle was still much tighter than it had to be as she stepped out of the car and approached the automatic doors of the entrance.

The monitors in her mother's hospital room made the only noise Callie could hear when she cautiously opened the door and looked in. Liddy's head had been propped up with extra pillows, but her eyes were still closed.

"Mom?" Callie ventured softly, taking a few hesitant steps into the room.

Liddy's eyes fluttered open. She made a mumbling sound that Callie couldn't make out, so she crept closer and put one hand on her mother's bedside railing.

"Mom?" she repeated.

Liddy moved her head slightly to see Callie better. Her eyes had an unfocused look to them, as if the pain medication hadn't completely worn off, but she smiled as she recognized her daughter, and the delight on her face made Callie's heart constrict. "Callie? What are you doing here?" Her words came out slurred.

"Danny called. He told me about your accident."

"Accident?" She looked confused for a moment. "Oh, yes. Blasted ladder." She closed her eyes again.

Callie leaned closer. "The doctor says you'll be fine. You'll be taking it easy for several weeks, but don't worry about a thing. I'm going to be helping you out for a while. And I'll look after the store for you while you're laid up, okay?"

Liddy opened her eyes again. "Store? Yes. Get Debbie to help. And Danny.

Such a good boy."

As her mother drifted back to sleep, Callie sank down into a chair beside her bed. "He says hi," she said to the sleeping woman, who stirred briefly but didn't wake up. He had said a lot of other things, too. Callie watched her mother doze and wondered what kinds of things he and Liddy spoke about. If her mother missed her as much as Danny said, why hadn't she ever said as much to her?

Because she was stubborn, no doubt, Callie thought. Just like her. The apple didn't fall far from the tree.

But the pleasure on her mother's face at the sight of her just now had been unmistakable. Too bad it took a heavy anesthetic to remove her emotional inhibitions. It was a place to start, though, Callie thought as she leaned back in the chair and watched over Liddy's sleeping form. And maybe this time they could meet in the middle and she could get the answers she needed from her mother.

CHAPTER THREE

Her mother's pride and joy. Not Callie, the daughter in question thought wryly, but her mother's gift shop: Liddy's Little Treasures. There were no mass-produced items to be found in here, only painstakingly handcrafted oddities made by local artists. Liddy was a big believer in supporting the local economy. Even the sign bearing the shop's name had been handmade, and from a tree that had grown not far from here. There was a history behind every single piece in the place.

There was also a lot of dust.

Callie crouched on her hands and knees with a feather duster and brushed dust and cobwebs off a row of wooden carvings of bears in hoop skirts on the bottom shelf. Clearly *these* little treasures were not hot items. Stifling a sneeze, she moved on to the next row. "Debbie," she called back over her shoulder. "Why don't we move those candlesticks over here instead? These bears have been sitting here so long that people have probably forgotten they exist. Let's move them front and center for a while and see what happens. Mom can always change it back if she doesn't like it." Besides, the bears were kind of appealing. Maybe someone would give at least one or two of them a happy home.

Her mother's lone employee peered around the corner of the shelves and adjusted her glasses, radiating disapproval. "Your mother doesn't really like other people to rearrange her things," the middle-aged woman said nervously.

"Then it'll just be added incentive for her to get better quickly, won't it?" Callie grunted, straining to move a wolf that had been sculpted out of aluminum cans a few inches further to the left where it was less likely to be tripped over.

"I, well—"

Callie gave her an exasperated look.

"Fine." Debbie disappeared, presumably to gather up the candlesticks or maybe to jot down a note on Callie's interference for some future report to Liddy. Callie had a feeling she had given her plenty of material already.

Standing up, Callie surveyed her handiwork. It would do. The store, which had been closed since her mother's accident, was neat and tidy again, and the damage caused by the falling ladder had been swept away. Callie had even created a new display in the front window to take the place of the half-finished one her mother had been working on when she fell. At its center was a little wooden mountain man with crutches and a cast on his leg, relaxing in his gnarled old rocking chair. Debbie had eyed her warily when she had seen it.

"I know," Callie had said, unperturbed. "Sick sense of humor. But Mom will laugh when she sees it, so what does that say about her, I ask you? I'm just a product of my environment."

She checked her watch. It was time to go back to the hospital. Her mother had had an entire night and half a day to sleep off any lingering effects of the anesthesia, so they would finally be able to have a genuine conversation. Callie had mixed feelings about that.

But there was one last quick thing to do before she left the store. Slapping a Help Wanted sign in the window, she taped its edges down securely.

There was a gasp behind her, and she turned to see Debbie staring at her in horror, her arms full of candlesticks. "But . . . your mother never—"

"I can't be here *and* at home to look after Mom at the same time," Callie pointed out reasonably. "And you need someone to split the shifts with, unless you want to move in to this place. Look, it doesn't have to be permanent or anything. Just hang on to any applications that get turned in, and I'll handle the rest—including Mom. Fair enough?"

Debbie nodded stiffly, brow furrowed with obvious displeasure.

"I've got to get to the hospital. Will you be okay to finish the afternoon without me?"

The other woman nodded again, her expression still sour, and Callie reminded herself to be patient. Not everyone handled change well, after all, and Debbie clearly depended on her routines. Callie gave her a comforting pat on the shoulder as she left. The poor woman nearly jumped a mile.

Callie's grip on the steering wheel got tighter the closer she got to the hospital. It wasn't that she didn't want to see Liddy; she loved her mother. But it was a well-documented fact that most mothers and daughters drove each other crazy more often than not, and Liddy and Callie were proof positive of that. The conversation between them would start out innocently enough, but sooner or later it would veer into uncomfortable territory. She'd bet good money on sooner.

As she parked the car and headed in toward her mother's room, she searched her mind for safe opening lines that wouldn't immediately lead to questions about her life's choices.

Her mind drew a blank, so she went with a tried and true classic as she walked through the door: "Hi, Mom."

Liddy looked up from a magazine she was reading to where her daughter stood in the doorway. "Callie," she greeted her, putting down the magazine and sounding more than a little surprised.

Callie ventured a little further into the room but kept a guarded distance. She found a safe spot across the room from her mother and leaned against a wall for support. "You look more like yourself today. Feeling better?"

"Fair enough under the circumstances, I suppose. The nurse said you stopped by last night. I must have been doped to the gills, because I don't remember a thing. Did we talk?"

"Not a lot. You weren't saying much that made sense. You would have made a terrific poster child for a 'Don't Do Drugs' campaign."

"No doubt."

They eyed each other warily for a moment, and then Liddy gestured at the chair by her bed. "Sit down, honey. No need to lurk in the corner when there's a perfectly good chair."

"Lurk, huh?" But Callie sat down as requested and fidgeted with the hem of her shirt. It had been months since they had talked, and years since they had seen each other face-to-face. Surely she could come up with something better to say than sarcasm and idle chit chat. She tried again. "So, Debbie's pretty interesting."

Apparently she couldn't.

"You've been to the store then?"

"Yes. Things are up and running again. You're going to need an extra body around there to help run the show while your hip is mending. I'm working on it."

"Thank you."

"No problem."

Several moments went by, during which neither of them spoke. Finally Liddy reached out and took Callie's hand in hers. She squeezed it gently. "How are you, Callie?"

Callie cleared her throat. "Good, Mom. I'm good." She squeezed her mom's hand back before releasing it and speaking with more lightness than she felt. "I haven't fallen off any ladders lately, at least."

"I'm not going to live this one down, am I?"

"Nope. Better just accept it now."

"When did you get into town, honey?"

"Yesterday. Danny called me."

"I'm sorry you had to come all this way. He shouldn't have troubled you with all of this."

"Yes, he should," Callie returned firmly. "You're my mother. Who else should he have called?"

She thought Liddy's eyes looked watery for a second, but the older woman blinked quickly, and they returned to normal. "It's just . . . I hate to be a bother. I'm sure I'd be able to figure something out on my own."

"You broke your hip, Mom. Like it or not, you're going to have to take it easy for a while and let other people help you, including me."

"Just because the doctors say I need babying—"

"The doctor said *weeks*, Mom," Callie said doggedly, leaning forward and giving her mother a stern look. "Several of them. Probably longer if you insist on being difficult. Don't expect to be doing anything except watching a lot of TV and catching up on your reading until the doctor gives you permission."

Her mother made a face. "Bah. They're just being overly cautious because they don't want to risk getting sued for malpractice. I'll be up and about before then."

"No, you won't. You're going to do exactly what the doctor says."

"Bossy, aren't you?"

Callie shrugged and leaned back in the chair. "Yeah, well . . ."

But her mother didn't look too displeased by Callie's insistence, and this time it was Liddy who had to clear her throat to cover up emotion. "It will be nice to have you visit for a while, though."

"You might want to reserve judgment on that until you taste my cooking."

"Hmm. There's always take-out." Liddy peered at her daughter more closely, until Callie began to feel self-conscious. "You look thin. Are you eating enough?"

"Yes."

"Are you sure? Living in that big city, I wonder when the last time was that you had a decent home-cooked meal."

They were veering into risky territory. Callie decided it might be wise to make an exit while things were still pleasant between them. She stood up. "I should get going—"

Her mother put a hand on her arm to stop her. "Oh, don't go yet. Danny's on his way over. We can all visit."

Callie stiffened. "Danny's coming?" She was not prepared to run into him again so soon.

"He called a little while ago and said he would stop by on his lunch break. Now that you're back in town, you two can catch up." Her mom gave her a delighted smile.

"We caught up a little already. I should really go. I'll come by tomorrow, okay?" She started for the door only to have it open just as she got there.

Danny stood on the other side of it, and he looked about as excited to see Callie there as she was to see him.

"Hi," she said uncertainly.

His expression was guarded. "Hi."

"Danny!" Liddy called out from behind Callie. "Perfect timing. Two minutes later, and you might have missed Callie."

"Imagine that," Callie murmured.

He heard her, judging by the way his eyes flickered briefly in her direction. "Yes, that is good timing, isn't it?" He walked past her to give Liddy a kiss on the cheek. "Hey, Liddy. You're looking better already."

She patted his cheek with one hand. "Thanks. The doctor thinks I might be able to go home by the end of next week. Personally, I think I could go home sooner, but I'll bet they're making a mint of money off my hospital stay. You think you might be able to help cart an old lady and her walker home?"

"I can do that, Mom," Callie said quickly. "No need to bother Danny."

Danny gave her a look that might have been tinged with amusement, as if he knew exactly why she was protesting. "It's no bother."

"Honey, I think it might be better to have Danny bring me home, just in case I'm not very steady and need someone to catch me. You understand, don't you?"

"Of course." But she could feel her face turning red. Callie looped her purse strap up and over her shoulder. "I really am going to get going this time. I'll see you later, Mom. Bye, Danny." And she made her escape.

Or at least she thought she did, but his voice stopped her before she got very far down the hall. "Callie."

She turned, tensing up.

He closed the distance between them slowly, almost reluctantly, and with each step he took, her tension grew. To her relief, he stopped when he was still a few feet away from her. "Look, about yesterday . . ."

She waited, holding her breath.

"Don't think I'm not glad you're home. Okay?"

"Okay."

He looked as if he wanted to say something more, but then thought better of it. "I'll see you," he said finally, turning to go back in to Liddy.

It was a small olive branch, but she would have to be a fool not to grab onto it with both hands. "Danny?" she said quickly, unwilling to let the fleeting moment of warmth end so soon.

"Yes?"

"Thanks for everything you've done for Mom."

"It's Liddy," he said, shrugging it off. "Of course I'd help."

"Still . . . thanks."

He nodded, and she watched him walk back the way he had come. Lame, she thought sourly at herself. She should have said something more. But of all the people she had ever met, he was the one who had always left her most at a loss for words. At least for words that really mattered.

*

The end of next week came, along with the doctor's approval, and Danny was as good as his word. Up until now, Callie had managed to avoid any more awkward encounters with him by immersing herself in Liddy's shop and only stopping by the hospital in the middle of the day when Danny was likely to be guiding tourists down the river. Now, awkward as it was, she was going to have to figure out a way to make conversation with him. As she waited for him to pull into the driveway with her mother, Callie restlessly rearranged furniture downstairs to make it easier for her mother to maneuver, rolling up area rugs and clearing wide paths for a walker.

She stacked an armload of books and magazines beside her mother's bed, enough to keep her busy for months, let alone weeks. For a moment she considered including a copy of a magazine that had printed one of Callie's pieces . . . No, she decided finally, wistful. There was a reference in it about Callie's father, vague but still a reference that Liddy would notice. This was not the time.

She turned her attention back to the task at hand and gave the bedroom a final appraisal. There was a television on top of the dresser, but no DVD player. Maybe Callie could figure out how to hook one up before Liddy got bored and tried to get out of bed before she was supposed to do so. Knowing her mother, she might just have to strap her down for her own good, and then possibly sit on her.

The sound of tires on gravel made her look out the window. They were here. Taking a deep breath, she went out to meet them, still self-conscious about Danny being there despite the tenuous way they had made up. As he turned the engine off and got out of the driver's side, Callie opened the door and helped her mother swivel around in her seat.

"Thank you, honey. I think I've got it now. Danny'll bring the walker around."

"I still think we could have managed just fine on our own," Callie murmured to her mother, her eyes on Danny as he retrieved the walker from the back of his truck. The sun had left natural highlights in his sandy hair, and she caught herself staring first at them and then at the bronzed skin of his forearms.

"Don't be silly," her mother said. "He doesn't mind helping."

Callie averted her eyes and spoke more briskly than she intended. "That's not what I—it's just that he has a business to run, Mom. We shouldn't take him away from it any more than we have to."

"He does have other river guides working for him, Callie. I mean, what's the point of being the boss if you can't take a little time off from work now and then, right, Danny?"

Danny appeared in the open door in time to hear the last part of their exchange. "Sure," he said agreeably. "Why?"

"Callie says I shouldn't have called you."

Biting back a retort, Callie felt her face grow warm.

He glanced at her. "She does, does she?"

"But I knew you wouldn't mind. You're a good boy, Danny." Liddy took the arm he offered and poked her good leg out the door. "I don't know what I'd do without you." Using her new walker for support but relying mainly on Danny, Liddy stood up. "Oh," she breathed, wincing at first but then looking at her house. "It is so good to be home."

Avoiding Danny's eyes, Callie turned back to the house. "I'll get the door," she said shortly.

She held the front door wide open as Danny assisted Liddy up the front walk. He took such care with her mom, and despite the tension between him and Callie, she was touched. Her mother had taken it for granted that he would be there when she asked him to, and apparently she had good reason to do so. Maybe that was one reason why Callie had felt free to leave home years ago, because she knew Danny would be there. And maybe that had been unfair of her.

He helped Liddy into the bedroom, careful not to jostle her any more than necessary.

"Ah," she said with satisfaction, sinking down onto the bed. "This looks like a place I could settle into for a good six weeks or so. We'll call it rehab central."

Danny adjusted the many pillows Callie had arranged on the bed. "Okay?" he asked.

Liddy sighed with pleasure as she nestled back into the pillows. "Home," she breathed again. "Oh, my darling house, I'll never take you for granted again."

Callie brought a tray in from the kitchen with a glass of water and a plate of crackers and cheese. "Here," she said, placing it on a small folding table beside the bed. "There's fresh fruit in the fridge, too, if you'd like some."

"I may never want to get up from here," Liddy told her happily, surveying her little domain and examining the selection of books Callie had set out for her. "Throw in a personal masseur, and I'm set. You've thought of just about everything, haven't you?"

"Except dinner," Callie said, glancing at her watch. "I'll go heat up something up, if you want. I've lost count of the number of people who have stopped by to drop off casseroles. You're set for food for the next couple of years, I think." It had been rather amazing to see all of the people who had appeared out of the woodwork to offer their support if Liddy should need it. Touching, even. Having roots did have some advantages after all.

But her mother shook her head. "Oh, no. I'm really not that hungry. I'll just have a yogurt or something. But you two— Danny, would you humor an old lady and take Callie out for a decent meal? I'll bet she's had nothing but take-out and leftovers since she's been here."

Callie stiffened. The two of them out for dinner? Alone? She wasn't sure if she was ready for that. Their fragile truce might not survive it. "I'm fine, Mom, really. I like leftovers. Anyway, I don't want to leave you—"

"I insist. I'll be absolutely fine, honey. See? I've got the phone right here if I need to have you hurry home. I just feel awful that you had to drop everything and fly out here like this, and I know you've been working at the shop all week, too. You deserve a treat. Please, Danny?" Liddy fixed wide eyes upon him that would have melted the most hardened of hearts. There was even a slight quiver in her voice.

Callie frowned at her. It was a little over the top, and quite unlike her mother.

"Sure," Danny said, his face neutral. "You want us to bring you back something?"

"No, no. I'll probably just settle in for the night right here and be out like a light within no time. Don't hurry back on my account. I'll be fine." Liddy smiled brightly up at them and then yawned a yawn that seemed a little forced to Callie. "You two go out and catch up."

She could tell, Callie decided, that things were not right between her daughter and Danny, and this was her way of trying to fix it. There was no graceful way to get out of it.

She looked at Danny, hoping the unease didn't show on her face.

His own face was unreadable as he gestured toward the door. "After you."

CHAPTER FOUR

It was clear that she didn't want to be here. She sat stiffly in her seat and looked everywhere else around the sports bar but at him.

"You can pretend to watch that baseball game if you want to," he said dryly, opening up his menu and looking it over, "but don't think for a minute that I'm buying it."

"What?" she returned. "Maybe I like baseball now. For all you know, I could be the Yankees' biggest fan."

"Fine," he said without looking up. "Then tell me what a ground rule double is."

She mulled it over. "Oh, shut up," she muttered finally.

He grinned at her then, unable to help himself, and she reddened. But she smiled a little, too. He felt a sweet stab of pleasure at the sight and told himself not to ruin things by saying anything else.

Their waitress stopped by their table and turned her attention immediately to Danny. "Ready to order?"

"Steak," Danny said. "Medium rare."

"The same," Callie echoed. "And a side order of onion rings."

"Anything to drink?"

"A beer." He glanced at Callie.

"Make that two."

The waitress upped the wattage of her smile, and Danny returned it politely but only for a moment, and she left. "Quite the appetite," he observed. "I remember you as more of a soup and salad kind of person."

"There's a lot you don't know about me anymore."

"I suppose so. It's a little unnerving."

"Really?"

"Don't look so pleased."

She smiled again, and he felt a little more of the tension between them melt away.

"So tell me," he asked, careful to keep his voice casual, "what else don't I know about you now?"

Their waitress delivered their beers and the onion rings, smiling coyly at Danny again. "Anything else I can get you?"

"Thanks," Callie said with a pointed stare. "We're good now." She waited until the other woman left before answering Danny's question. "Hmm. Let me think . . . I'm unemployed now."

He nearly choked on his first swallow of beer. "What?"

She shrugged in an apparent lack of concern and sampled an onion ring. "My choice. I'll find something else when I'm ready."

"When you're ready?" He thought he felt his blood pressure rise on the spot. Did she not have a practical bone in her body? "Callie, jobs aren't just—"

"Have an onion ring," she interrupted, thrusting one into his open mouth.

"Callie—"

"And don't talk with your mouth full. It's rude."

How could she make him want to shake her and laugh with her at the same time? He considered himself to be a laid-back sort of person, but she brought out tension in him that he hadn't even known existed. No one else made him worry quite like she did.

She took a drink and leaned back in her chair. "What else . . . I'm addicted to salsa."

"The condiment?"

"The dance. Oh, and I've been mugged a couple of times."

"You were *mugged*? Why didn't you tell anybody?"

"Oh, come one. You haven't truly experienced New York City until you've been mugged," she said. "And I've got a tattoo, a pimp, and a coke habit, too."

"*What?*" He watched as a wicked grin spread across her face, and his eyes narrowed. "You little sadist. Was any of that true, or was it all BS?"

"The tattoo part was true."

Picking up his beer, he put it to his lips to stop himself from asking where the tattoo was. Bad enough that images were already popping into his mind of inked artwork in intimate places. He took a long drink and tried to clear his head but found it difficult. She was teasing him, goading him because she was still irritated that he had not kept his opinions to himself about her choices. He shouldn't let her bait him.

"Couldn't resist," she said, pushing the basket of onion rings closer so that he could help himself. "You're so convinced that New York is this den of iniquity that's going to swallow me up."

"I didn't say that."

"You didn't have to. I know you, Danny. You still think of me as some little-girl-lost, but I'm all grown up now."

That she was. There were certainly flickers of the girl he used to know. Same independence, same devilish sense of humor. But there was something . . . *harder* about her. He guessed it came from living on her own since she was barely old enough to do so. When she'd first left, he'd had many restless nights spent wondering about all the people out there who wouldn't hesitate to take advantage of a beautiful young girl, and he felt that he had let Elliot and Liddy down in some way by not finding a way to convince her to stay. "You certainly grew up fast," he said finally.

She eyed him from across the table. Maybe she was trying to figure out if there was some sort of implied criticism in his words. He hadn't intended any. It was just difficult for him to figure out how to relate to her now. Somehow a stand-in for her big brother didn't seem to fit anymore, if it ever had. He would have to figure out something new.

"So, you love New York," he said, changing the subject.

"Love is a strong word. The city has charm, though."

"You've been there a while now. You planning on making it permanent, then?"

Her expression became wary. "I don't want to fight with you, Danny."

"I don't want to fight either."

"Then let's not get into it again. I'm here to help Mom out for a while, and then I'm heading back to New York. I don't know how long I'll stay or what I'll do after that, and I like it that way. You think I'm crazy, I know, or a flake, but I've just got a different perspective on life than you do."

Danny leaned back and folded his arms across his chest. "Enlighten me."

"All right. When's the last time you threw caution to the winds and just did something crazy? Felt some instinct tug at you and just . . . went for it? Can you even remember?" She leaned forward. "I'll bet you can't. You've had a plan for your whole life figured out since you were a teenager. And that may be fine for you, but not for me."

Her dark eyes lit up as she talked, and he found himself unable to look away as she continued.

"If I want to take off and backpack across Europe or hop a boat to China, I can do that because I'm not tied down. I know you thought it was a huge mistake when I decided to forget about college and head to LA, but I've never regretted it. What I would have regretted was living a life someone else picked out for me instead. I'm only twenty-four years old, Danny, and I've already done and seen some things that most people never will."

"I know."

She looked at him in surprise. "What do you mean?"

"I saw the piece you wrote a few years ago about the bayous. And the one you wrote about that old shopkeeper in Atlanta. The one from Saudi Arabia." They had been well written, understated but moving. They had also been a way for him to get a glimpse into her life even though she was miles away. And when he'd finished reading them, he had saved the magazines in which they were printed.

"You saw those?"

"Your mom let me know about them. They were good, Callie."

There was a faint blush in her cheeks. Self-conscious, she turned her attention to her onion rings, sweeping some of her dark hair behind one ear when it threatened to fall forward into her face. A few years ago she'd clipped it short, no-nonsense. The longer length suited her better, he thought, all soft and silky. He felt an urge to slide it between his fingers and find out for himself just how soft it was. Stifling the thought, he picked up his beer again instead and wondered if he had had too much to drink or not enough to be thinking such thoughts.

There had been another article that he had read, a couple of years ago, that he would be wise not to bring up now. She had written it not long after she had moved north, and it was about the differences between men and women. It, too, had been well written, but he thought that he had read something else between the lines. There had been a man somewhere along the line, and a bad break-up. He had no idea over what, but it had left her raw. Liddy hadn't known about that piece. Danny had found it himself, and it had been hard for him to read. Partly because of the hurt she seemed to be feeling. And partly . . . well, partly he wasn't sure.

He cleared his throat. "I don't doubt you've done some major living, Callie. I just don't think you need to live all the way across the country to do it."

"How would you know? You've never tried it."

"I've seen more of the outside world than you think."

"Really? When?"

But that was not something he was prepared to talk about, with her or with anyone. He kept silent, feeling Callie's questioning eyes on him.

Their waitress returned with their steaks, a welcome distraction.

*

Dinner was rather quiet after that. Danny kept his attention mostly on his steak, and the few times he looked up, Callie thought his eyes seemed distant. Their waitress, she noted, did not seem put off by that in the slightest and kept coming around to their table to refill water glasses that didn't need refilling. Callie shouldn't have minded since she and Danny were only there as friends, but the waitress could not have known that. The young woman tossed her blonde hair around and leaned forward in a blouse that Callie was fairly certain had been buttoned a couple of buttons higher when they had first sat down. It irritated her more than it should have.

"You have got to try the mud pie," the woman urged Danny, not even pretending to care about Callie now. "I can't let you leave here without a taste of something sweet."

Callie choked on her last bite of steak, then recovered. "Just the check will be fine."

She could have sworn the other woman's eyes narrowed slightly in her direction before refocusing on Danny. "Maybe you should let *him* decide what he wants," she suggested, leaning forward a little bit more.

If Danny was aware of the tension simmering between the two women, or the cleavage being displayed, he gave no sign of it. "No, just the check, thanks," he said, glancing up only briefly from the table.

Callie grinned at the waitress.

The blonde scowled back and left.

Relaxing back into her chair, Callie watched Danny. She was both embarrassed and pleased that he had seen the articles she had written and had liked them. How her mother had found about them in the first place, Callie didn't know. She hadn't mentioned her writing any of the few times she had called her mom, preferring to keep the details of her life to herself. Maybe she wanted to avoid the possibility of parental disapproval. More likely it had been a way to get back at Liddy for withholding a few details herself, she thought with a flicker of guilt.

Across from her, Danny sighed heavily. She looked at him, startled, and realized he wasn't even aware he had done it. Something was weighing on him, and she thought it must be more than Liddy's accident or Callie's lifestyle. She was ashamed to realize that she had no idea what was going on in his life now. It was her own fault, since she had virtually broken off all contact with home. She reached out to touch his hand. "Something wrong?"

He jerked his hand back as if she had burned him. She tried not to let it bother her. Some people were just private, that was all, and she should respect that. Wasn't she like that herself?

"Maybe we should have ordered some of that mud pie to go," he said with false lightness instead of answering her question. "For your mom. I know what she said, but I doubt she'd turn it down."

She tried to match his casual tone. "Too late. Check's here."

The blonde slid their check in front of Danny and favored him with one last smile.

"Come back soon," she said over her shoulder as she moved on to another table.

As Danny reached into his wallet for some cash, Callie glanced at the check. Her mouth fell open. "Of all the nerve!"

"What?" he asked, glancing up in confusion.

Wishing she had kept her mouth shut, Callie just shook her head and got up from her chair.

Danny leaned forward to get a closer look at the check. "Oh," he said, dawning comprehension in his voice. "Her phone number." He looked up at Callie. "You disapprove?"

"Well, for all she knows, you and I could be out on a date!"

"Mm. But we're not, right?"

"She doesn't know that." She heard the annoyance in her voice and forced it out. "I just think it's tacky is all," she said with an indifferent shrug. She pulled enough cash from her wallet to cover her meal. "Are you coming?"

"Tacky," he repeated, appearing to consider her words. He fingered the check thoughtfully. "So you think I shouldn't take it, then? I mean, if she's so tacky."

"Hey, whatever floats your boat. Here's my share of the check." He shook his head. "I've got it."

"I insist. I wouldn't want you to think I was a mooch as well as a flake. I'm going to the ladies' room. Give you time to make your move on Blondie over there." Looping the straps of her purse over her shoulder, she departed for the restroom without a backward glance, even though a part of her was dying to see if he actually did approach the waitress.

She pushed open the restroom door and braced herself against the sink, staring at herself in the mirror. *What is wrong with you?* she mouthed at her reflection. Her cheeks were flushed and her dark eyes flashed back at her. There was no reason for her to be snippy with Danny, and she certainly had no right to offer opinions on his love life. He could date whomever he chose. For all she knew, he was seeing somebody already and she had been so preoccupied with her own life that she had neglected to ask him.

Could he be seeing someone? It was only natural that he should. She would be lying to herself if she said she hadn't been wondering about it since the phone call he'd gotten back at the house her first day back. As their waitress had proved tonight, he was the kind of guy to catch a girl's eye. Why wouldn't he have someone special in his life? She was embarrassed that the thought left a bitter taste in her mouth. Had she really expected him to live like a monk for the rest of his life so he could be at her or her mom's beck and call? That was hardly fair.

She felt a flicker of panic that surprised her, and she did her best to smother it without examining it too closely. This was Danny, after all. True, she had carried a torch for him when she was younger, but he didn't know anything about that. As far as he knew he was just a friend, and that's all he had ever been. A good friend, but one she had left behind her in her pursuit of . . . what, exactly?

She frowned and peered more intently in the mirror. Life? The thrill of the open road? That was what she had told him earlier, but lately she wasn't entirely convinced. There was something else she was looking for. Maybe the same thing her father had been looking for.

An image came to her mind, hazy around the edges, of her father holding her hand as they walked through the local park. It had been so long since she had seen a picture of him that the features of his face were vague and indistinct. Her heart constricted, and she turned away.

Coming home had stirred up memories and emotions long buried. If she was acting like a jealous teenager around Danny, it was probably because of that. He had been all she thought about for much of her adolescence, and being back home was simply stirring up echoes of feelings that were no longer there. That was all. It was a reasonable explanation.

He was waiting for her when she came out, leaning casually against the doorframe of the exit and looking out at the cars in the parking lot. Callie faltered mid-step but collected herself before he saw her. Those memories of her teenage crush were awfully vivid right now. She tried to shake them off as she approached him.

"Ready?" he asked. When she nodded, he held the door open and gestured for her to go first. "After you."

She stole a quick glance in the direction of their table but couldn't tell if he had taken the waitress's phone number with him or left it lying there. It was none of her business anyway, she told herself as she slid into the passenger's seat of Danny's truck.

As he started the engine, he pulled some cash out of his pocket and tucked it into Callie's purse.

"What are you doing?" she demanded. "I said I'd pay for my own dinner."

"You're unemployed now, remember? Keep it."

Her frustration mounted. "I'm not destitute, Danny! I quit my job to come take care of Mom, not because they fired me or anything—"

"You quit your job to come here? Because I called you?"

"My jerk of a boss wouldn't give me the time off. It's no big deal. I'll have another job within a week of getting back, no problem. I always land on my feet."

"Damn, Callie. If I had known you would do that, I would have thought twice before calling," he said ruefully.

"Why? Mom would still need someone to help take care of her, and you can only take off so much time from work. Besides, isn't 'family first' the motto you want me to adopt anyway?" She held the cash out to him. "Here. I'm doing just fine, really."

"No."

"Just take it."

"No."

"Danny, I swear—" Muttering under her breath, she tried to shove the money back into the pocket of his jeans.

He caught her hand with his. "Careful, Callie. One wrong slip of the hand, and you should be the one buying *me* dinner."

She realized then just exactly where her hand was and what he meant. "You idiot," she said, unable to keep from laughing and trying not to blush. "Fine. I'll keep the money. This time. But I make no promises about your maidenly virtue next time."

A slow grin spread across his face and she felt sixteen again and unable to form coherent thoughts. He was so beautiful. No wonder the waitress had made a play for him. She would be crazy not to.

He released her hand and she clasped it in her other one, safely out of temptation's way in her lap. She was not sixteen anymore, although it felt good to laugh with him like she used to do. She was only visiting, and in a while, she would be moving on again. "Thanks for dinner," she said, facing forward once more.

He would have walked her to the front door when they got to Liddy's house, she was sure, but Callie hastened out of the truck before he could get his own door open. She was too giddy around him for her liking and felt a need to put some space between them. "Thanks again," she said with an overly cheerful wave. "I'll tell Mom you made sure I was well-fed, as ordered." She turned to go up the front walk.

"Callie?"

She turned back. "Yes?"

Whatever he was about to say, he changed his mind. "Nothing. Say good night to your mom for me."

"I will."

His truck's engine roared to life again and then faded into the distance as he drove off. It was what she had wanted, but mass of contradictions that she was, she was sorry to see him go.

Liddy was still comfortably ensconced in her bedroom when Callie walked through the front door. The television was on, but she muted it when she heard her daughter. Her voice drifted out to the living room. "Back so soon? I thought you might want to make a night of it. How was dinner?"

"Fine," Callie called out, tossing her purse onto the couch. "How's your leg?"

"Oh, as good as can be expected. I can't say I'm overly fond of the exercises they gave me to do, though. Oh, well. I took another pain pill about an hour ago, and it's starting to kick in."

"Hungry?"

"I wouldn't say no to a snack."

Rummaging through the cupboards, Callie pulled out a bag of microwave popcorn and put it into the microwave.

"I hope you kids didn't cut things short on my account," her mother called into the kitchen. "I had hoped you two would get a chance to catch up. It's been so long, after all."

Callie leaned in the bedroom doorway and gave her mother a knowing look. "You mean you were meddling. You guilted Danny into taking me out to dinner because you were trying to 'fix' things."

Liddy was unrepentant. "It's a mother's right to meddle when it's in her child's best interest. What's going on between you two anyways?"

"Same old, same old. He thinks I'm making all the wrong choices. I think they're my choices to make. You two aren't planning some sort of intervention, are you?"

"Why, yes, dear. And step one of our diabolical little plan was to have me break my hip in order to get you on a plane. I'd say everything is coming together rather neatly, wouldn't you?"

"You're getting sarcastic in your old age."

"I was born sarcastic, honey."

The microwave timer went off, and Callie returned to the kitchen to dump the steaming popcorn into a bowl for her mother.

Her mother's voice followed her. "So did you two sort everything out?"

"What's to sort out? He's got his opinions, and I've got mine. Extra butter?"

"Yes, please. I mean, are you two on friendly terms again, or am I going to have to break my other leg?"

Callie delivered the bowl of popcorn to her mother. "Don't push it, Mother." She took a deep breath. "There's something else I want to talk to you about anyway."

Liddy took a handful of popcorn. "What is it?"

"Dad."

Her mother's hand froze in midair between the bowl and her mouth.

"I'm not a child anymore, Mom. I have a right to make decisions for myself, including whether or not I get to know my father."

Liddy put the bowl of popcorn down, her face grave. "Callie—"

There was a "no" coming, but she wasn't going to take no for an answer anymore. "It's a sore subject for you, I get that. And you probably think you're protecting me. I get that, too. But . . ." She sat on the edge of her mother's bed, her eyes imploring. "I don't even have a picture of him, Mom. You wouldn't let me keep even that much of him."

Her mother's face grew sad, and she touched Callie's cheek softly. "You don't understand, honey."

"No, I don't understand, and I'm tired of it. There's this whole other part of me that I feel I don't know. I need to find him, Mom. I need your help. You wouldn't help me before, but I'm asking you again. Please."

"Finding your father won't help you, Callie. You're better off without him. Whatever you're looking for, can't you try to find it here?"

"I don't belong here."

"You could if you tried."

"Mom—"

Sighing, Liddy let her head sink back into the pillows. "I've got a terrible headache, honey. Would you get me an ice pack, please?"

Callie's shoulders slumped in frustration. She had expected as much, but if her mother thought she would give up that easily this time, she was mistaken. "Yes, Mom. I'll get you an ice pack, and I'll stay long enough to help you get back on your feet. But if you want this—us—to work, it can't just be on your terms."

She turned and went back into the kitchen to wrap some ice in a towel for her mom. Her eyes were stinging, and she touched them in surprise to find them wet. She hated arguing with her mother, hated running up against a brick wall every time she tried to get through to her. The last time she had been home had been the worst. She had no illusions; her father had abandoned them. She was not expecting to find a saint, but she still needed to find him. Her mother just couldn't seem to understand that.

Drying her eyes, Callie regained her composure. "Here," she said, returning to the bedroom and holding out the ice pack.

Liddy took it and pressed it to her temple. "Thank you."

"I'm not giving up, Mom."

Her mother closed her eyes. "No. I know you aren't."

*

Callie sat alone in her old room, trying again without success to conjure up an image of her father. She thought he must have been kind to her because she felt a wistful sort of affection when she thought of him, but it was impossible to tell how much of that was just wishful thinking on her part. Impossible without help, at least. Help that her mother had refused to give her over the years.

Seeking an outlet for her frustration, she reached for her notebook.

Most people think that coming home is like the ultimate feeling of belonging. Everything is as it should be when you're finally home again. Parts of yourself come together like pieces in a jigsaw puzzle, and everything fits. But for some people, coming home is only a reminder that you don't have all the pieces you need, and without them it's hard to make sense of the rest.

I wish I could make the pieces fit.

CHAPTER FIVE

" . . . extra rolls of receipt paper are in the back room if you run out. There are extra bags back there, too. Our home phone number is right here if something should pop up that you have a question about. And . . . I think that's everything. Any questions?"

The young woman standing before Callie in Liddy's gift shop smiled brightly and shook her head. "Nope, I think I've got it. Thanks again for the job. I can use a little extra income this summer."

"Great. Works out well for everybody, then." Callie held up a key. "Here's your copy of the store key. The back door sticks a little, but not too badly. Welcome aboard, Allyson. We're all glad to have you."

From behind her somewhere, Debbie muttered something under her breath that Callie chose to ignore.

A cuckoo clock on the wall announced the time as twelve o'clock. "That's my cue," Callie said. "Mom needs her lunch. Like I said, any questions—any that Debbie here can't answer, I mean—just give me a call."

On her way out the front door, she pulled the Help Wanted sign off the window.

Her mother had had an astonishing number of visitors since her accident, most of whom came bearing gifts of casseroles or offers of help with errands and other things, so it didn't surprise Callie to see another vehicle parked in the driveway at Liddy's house. What did surprise her was that it was Danny's truck. He hadn't said anything to her about coming by today.

She felt her pulse speed up and told herself she was being silly. Still, she caught herself doing a quick check of her appearance

60

in the rearview mirror. Knock it off, she warned herself before grabbing her things and getting out of the car.

Danny came out through the front door just as Callie started down the walkway. "Hi," she greeted him awkwardly. "I didn't know you'd be here." That hadn't come out right at all, she thought, kicking herself mentally. Could she have made him feel any less welcome?

"Just dropping off a few groceries."

"Oh. Thanks."

"But I've got a group scheduled at one, so I'll get out of your way here." He made as if to go around her.

"You're not in my way," she said quickly, putting a hand on his arm to stop him. She removed it just as hastily, afraid that he might sense the effect even such simple contact with him had on her. "I just meant that I was surprised. You've taken off so much time from work already to help Mom. I hope it hasn't been too inconvenient for you, is all."

"It's fine. Next week's booked pretty solid, though. It will be tough to get away then."

"Right. Your busy season and all." It was inane-sounding chitchat. She was much more comfortable with written words, she decided, than with spoken ones. At least with certain people.

"So . . ."

"Yeah, right. Tourists are waiting. Let me get out of *your* way." She stepped aside to give him room to pass. "Thanks again, Danny."

He shrugged off her thanks and put on a pair of sunglasses. "I'll see you."

As he walked to his truck, she toyed with a sudden impulse to ask him to dinner at the house. It was a perfectly normal thing to do with an old friend, so it shouldn't have been so hard. As old friends, why shouldn't they be able to enjoy each other's company during her visit?

But she couldn't seem to get the words out, so she watched him drive away instead before turning to go inside the house.

She had to laugh at herself. It was silly. He was a friend, nothing more, and there was no reason for her to feel self-conscious around him. It must just be the effect of having old memories stirred up of teenage crushes. There was nothing more to it than that.

Really.

But she still wondered if he had asked out that waitress.

*

"Honey, do me a favor?"

Callie put down the pot she was scrubbing. "What?"

Her mother waved a fistful of cash at her from the couch. "Danny dropped off some groceries the other day at lunch time, and I forgot to pay him back for them. Could you drop this off for me?"

"'Forgot,' huh?" she muttered under her breath. Then she raised her voice. "Can't you just give it to him the next time he comes by?"

"What if he needs it before then? I'd feel terrible if something came up, and he didn't have the money, and—"

"All right, all right," Callie conceded, knowing full well that she was being manipulated. "I'll drop it off by his house when I go into town later."

"He won't be there, he'll be working."

"His grandpa will be there, won't he? I can just leave it with him." While she had never heard any mention of Danny's parents in all the time she had known him, he had spoken of his grandfather many times and with obvious affection. She had only met the old man a few times, but she had a dim recollection of a tall man with white hair at Elliot's funeral, silent and stern looking. He'd said little to Liddy at the service, and even less to Callie, but he had offered Liddy his arm when she had begun to tremble, and his handkerchief when her tears had come.

For a moment, her mother was quiet. "I don't think that would be a good idea," she said finally. "Miles hasn't been up for visitors lately."

"Is he okay?"

Liddy smiled, but without cheer. "He's getting old, honey. Happens to the best of us."

So Callie found herself driving out to Danny's outfitter later that afternoon with a wad of cash and the uncomfortable thought that if she could tell this was a flimsy excuse to see Danny, he would likely think the same thing.

"It was Mom's idea," she said aloud in the car, and then laughed at herself. If she blurted that out as soon as she saw him, it would probably just make her look worse. She hadn't felt this self-conscious since . . . well, since the last time she saw Danny.

The conifers grew thicker as she turned off the highway and down a gravel road. She made a wrong turn once and had to go back, but for having been away so long, she was pleased with how well she remembered her way. The launch point for most of Danny's rafting trips was much further upstream, but the business itself was in a log cabin-style building not far from the river's edge. Callie pulled her mother's hatchback to a stop in the graveled lot and looked up through her sunglasses.

The building was bigger than she remembered, and it had been designed beautifully in that it seemed like it sprang from the woods naturally. A few other cars were in the lot, and she saw that Danny had expanded his business because there were two company vans now instead of one with boat trailers hooked up behind them and large rubber rafts in tow. The business logo "River's Edge Rafting Company" was emblazoned on the side of each vehicle, and Callie smiled as she remembered the hard time she had given Danny about the name years earlier.

"River's Edge Rafting, huh? Very creative. What, was Patch of Dirt Right Next to the Water Where We Float Boats already taken?" she had asked, holding the stencils in place as he painted the sign.

"Couldn't fit it on the letterhead," he had countered dryly. Then he had scooped her up and dunked her, laughing, in the river.

Maybe she had only been seventeen, but she thought she might have been a little bit in love with him then. And her teenage heart was broken because she had wanted so badly for him to kiss her that day, but he hadn't seemed to notice.

The sign was still there, mounted above the entrance. The sun and rain had weathered it a bit, but that only lent it charm. A rack with kayaks and canoes stood off to the side—it looked new. Business seemed to be going well.

Callie tucked her sunglasses into the neckline of her tank top and opened the door in time to hear a peal of feminine laughter. Her eyes adjusted to the natural lighting and focused immediately on a petite young brunette behind a desk, the only other person in the room. A door behind her that might have led to a storeroom was closed. The girl was on the phone, but she gestured to Callie that she was almost done, and Callie took the opportunity to look around inside the office.

There were some beautifully carved oars in one corner that could have been hung on the wall as art. She ran her fingers over them and marveled at how smooth they were. Her mother had probably put Danny in touch with a local craftsman.

A rack of pamphlets hung on the wall above a couple of wooden chairs along with framed evidence of proper certification. Next to them were several framed photographs. She took a step closer and recognized one of Elliot.

It was the one that had hung in her brother's room. That day eight years ago when she and Danny had worked side by side to pack up Elliot's things, Callie had given him the picture knowing he would appreciate it more than anyone else ever could.

And now it hung in the outfitter that had been the dream of both young men. It was fitting, she decided, her eyes misting. And touching.

"Can I help you?"

Callie turned around, blinking to rid her eyes of the tears that threatened. The brunette was off the phone and was hastily scribbling a note down on paper. "I'm looking for Danny McCutcheon. Is he here?"

The girl checked her watch, sunlight from the window glinting off highlighted streaks in her hair that looked more like they came from a salon than from the sun. "He should be back soon from the last trip. Do you want to wait, or is there something I can help you with?"

She could just leave the money and go. Then again, that might seem strange, to drive out all the way from town and not linger long enough to say hello. "I'll wait."

"Have a seat. Are you a friend of Danny's?"

Callie settled into one of the wooden chairs. "From years ago. Callie Sorenson?"

The girl looked blank and shrugged. "Danny doesn't talk about his personal life much. Great guy, though."

She was tempted to ask the girl how well she knew Danny, but was afraid it would come out sounding jealous. So she smiled through tight lips instead and waited silently while the receptionist got back to her paperwork.

When the front door opened, she nearly jumped. She was wound far too tightly lately. Danny walked in, his hair and clothes soaked from the river. "Sorry I'm late, Em," he told the girl, unaware of Callie's presence. "We had a little hang-up with one of the life vests. Wish I'd had my camera." He wrung some water from his shirt, and Callie caught the briefest glimpse of his back, muscled and tanned.

The girl, Em, pulled out a brown bag from a mini-fridge beside the desk and stood up. "No problem. I'm taking lunch down by the big rock today, if you need me." She nodded behind him on her way out the door. "You've got company, by the way."

Danny turned around and blinked in clear surprise. "Callie?"

The wet t-shirt clung to him like a second skin. Living and working on the river had chiseled him like few other things could. She swallowed, unable to think of something to say. "Mom asked me to come," she said finally, wincing inwardly. She thrust the handful of bills at him. "For groceries."

He stared at her with a bewildered look on his face, and then slowly reached out for the money. "You could have just given it to me the next time I came by."

"It was Mom's idea," she repeated, wanting to slap herself.

"So you said."

She stood up, fumbling awkwardly for words. "Well, I guess I should get out of your hair."

"Stay," he invited, gesturing toward the chair in which she had just been sitting. "I mean, you drove all this way. There's juice, if you want. Chips." He reached into the mini-fridge. "Apple okay?"

She took it from him, careful not to touch his fingers with her own. "Thanks."

Danny leaned back against the desk and took a long swig from his own bottle. "Sorry," he said, with a glance down at his drenched figure. "I'm a mess. Just came off the river. I've got another group coming in a few minutes." He gave her a speculative look, and she thought there was a glimmer of mischief in his face. "You up for a trip on the water while you're in town?"

"I hadn't thought about it."

"Let me know if you're interested."

There was a lull during which neither of them seemed to know where to look. "Mom seems to be doing well," Callie offered finally. "She's getting awfully good with that walker. She insisted on seeing the store yesterday."

"She see your window display?"

"Yep."

He grinned. "Did you get a dirty look?"

"Oh, yeah. Totally worth it." That smile of his was intoxicating. She got up from her chair in order to escape from it and wandered closer to the photos on the wall. "I see you kept it," she said, nodding toward the picture of her brother.

"It seemed like the best place for it."

"You've really turned this place into something great, Danny. Elliot would have loved it."

"Thank you. I think he would have liked it, too."

She heard emotion beneath his words and turned her head to look at him. He held her eyes with his, and she thought the distant look she'd seen so often in them lately faded.

One or both of them should have looked away by now, but neither did. She turned her body to face his more directly, her pulse speeding up. He watched her, his gaze never leaving hers, and she took a step closer. In another moment, she was going to do or say something stupid, she could feel it.

She was saved by the front door opening.

"Snyder, party of three, reporting for duty!" A stocky young man with a blonde crew cut and a bad sunburn staggered in through the door. "Let's get this freakin' thing started! Yeah!"

He hooted loudly, and was answered by the cheers of two other young men on the porch behind him. Then he stumbled and nearly fell before he caught himself with the door handle, laughing.

Callie's lip curled in disgust. They reeked of alcohol.

Danny had noticed, too. Although his expression was neutral, she saw the tension appear in him at once. He moved casually, but Callie knew it was no accident that he put his body between hers and the newcomers'.

"Can I help you?" he asked with a level look.

"You can if you run this joint. We're your one o'clock, buddy. And we are ready for a little whitewater action!" He cheered again, and his friends responded in a similar manner with a gesture that Callie associated with surfer dudes.

Tourists, she thought. Looking to live on the edge a little and full of plenty of liquid courage.

"You boys have been doing a little partying already, haven't you?" Danny said amiably, sizing them up. He put a hand on Callie's arm and gave her a barely perceptible shove in the direction of the back door while he pretended to look at some paperwork on the desk. "Yeah, here it is. One o'clock. Brian Snyder. That would be you?"

"Yes, it would." The jock's eyes lit on Callie. He grinned at her. "Hiya, sweetheart. What's your name?"

She did not smile back.

When Danny spoke again, his voice was cordial but firm. "I'm sorry, but I'm afraid I can't take you out today, fellas."

The man turned his attention back to Danny. "What?"

"I'd love to take you down the river, Mr. Snyder, but I can't do it unless everybody's sober. Too risky. Against the rules."

Brian Snyder's bloodshot eyes struggled to focus, and it took a few moments for Danny's words to register in his brain. "Huh? What do you mean?"

"I mean I can't take you out on the water when you've been drinking."

"But . . ." The man sounded like a petulant child. His lips even formed a pout. "We drove a long way for this!"

Drove. They had gotten behind the wheel like this? Memories flooded Callie's mind of the night Elliot had died, and her gaze darkened.

She glanced at Danny and saw the muscles of his hands twitch as if he was resisting the urge to form them into fists. He was resisting for her, she suspected, because these men were drunk and therefore unpredictable, and some drunks got mean. He motioned behind his back for her to leave, to go through the back door, wherever it led.

And go where? she thought. Who was she supposed to run to for help? Em? Callie had left her cell phone in her purse on the chair that was now effectively blocked by three angry men. It hardly seemed to matter. No cops would get here fast enough, even if she could call 911. If something were about to happen, it would be over long before they got there. Danny was trying his best to diffuse the situation before it really began, but it was too soon to tell if it was working or not. Brian Snyder was an awfully big man. So were his friends, she realized, as they stepped inside.

Did he really expect her to just run away and leave him?

*

Why wasn't she leaving? Danny cursed inwardly.

"Hey, man, we've been really lookin' forward to this," one of Snyder's friends protested, his voice slurring. "So we had a few beers. No big deal. Let's saddle up, amigo, and get going."

It was not the first time he had had to turn a customer away for being under the influence, but it was the first time he'd had someone else's safety to worry about besides his own. And of all people, it was Callie. Every muscle in his body felt taut. "Can't do it. Someone could get hurt. You guys don't want to spoil your day like that, do you? Ruin the buzz? Why don't you kick back and relax in the shade for a while instead. Take a dip in the water."

"You freakin' kidding me, man? We didn't come all the way out here to go *wading*." The man threw out a string of expletives.

Snyder got a knowing look in his eye and reached into his back pocket to pull out his wallet. "Okay, okay, I get it." He pulled out some cash and held it under Danny's nose. "How much more's it going to take to bend the rules, huh?"

"I don't bend the rules. Time to go." It was unlikely that he would be able to talk them into handing over their keys. He would have to call the cops once they were outside. They would get pulled over before they had a chance to hurt anyone. Right now he didn't want to set them off any more than necessary while Callie was in the room.

Snyder got right in Danny's face, staggering slightly with the effort to stand upright. "A real boy scout, aren't you?"

Danny stared back, his face like granite. The time for words was rapidly coming to an end. Why wasn't Callie getting out of there?

"Think you're too good for us?" Snyder's voice was low, which might be more dangerous than if he was shouting. "Lookin' down your nose at us. I've known your type my whole life. Think we're second-class. Punk." He glanced again at Callie. "You ought to come with us, sweetheart. We're a hell of a lot more fun than this guy." He tried to reach behind Danny as if to grab Callie's hand.

Danny's self-control snapped.

He grabbed Snyder by the collar and slammed him back into the man behind him, causing both men to stumble. "Get your hands off her, you drunken son of a bitch!"

The last man had enough reflexes left to jump out of the way, and now he bellowed and charged at Danny while his two friends tried to regain their footing.

"Callie, get out of here!" Then Danny grunted as the third man struck him headfirst in the chest and sent him careening back into the desk, and he had no chance to see if she did as he told her.

He hadn't been in many fights since he was a young kid; there hadn't been any need for it. Some of the reflexes came back to him, and he smashed his fist into the other man's throat hard enough to make him drop to his knees and gasp for breath. But Snyder was ready for him this time, and he threw a punch into Danny's face before he could block it.

The world was an explosion of light and stars. Going on instinct more than sight, Danny threw a punch of his own and connected with the other man's jaw, and then his gut. Then the sound of shattering glass made him wheel around to see the third man holding up the jagged end of a juice bottle.

The drunk took a menacing step forward.

Then he fell as a wooden paddle connected with the back of his head. Callie stood behind him, her eyes wide with anger and her lips in a hard line. She raised the paddle, ready to swing it again.

Snyder started toward Danny, then thought better of it. His gaze darted back and forth between Callie's paddle and Danny's fists.

"Your keys," Danny said, tasting blood in his mouth. "Leave them. You're walking back to town."

The other man's face turned purple. "You can't—"

"Leave them!"

Cursing, Snyder pulled a key ring from his pocket and flung it on the floor.

Danny picked them up. "You'll find your car in the empty lot at Third and Plum tomorrow, after you've sobered up. Keys'll be under the front seat. And then you'd better go back wherever you came from, because if I see your car in town again, I'll call the cops."

The man he had punched in the throat had finally gotten some air back, but the fight had gone out of him. He stooped over the one Callie had knocked out and began to haul him upward.

Brian Snyder finally made a good decision and helped the other two back out the door. Danny followed them out onto the porch and watched as they stumbled down the road in the direction of the highway.

"Stupid fools could kill somebody." He spat blood onto the ground and flexed his hand. The knuckles were bleeding.

"Are you all right?" Callie's voice was shaky.

He turned around to see her standing in the open doorway. "I'm fine. You?"

She nodded.

Unconvinced, he cupped her chin in his good hand and tilted her head to one side and then the other to check for any cuts or bruises.

"I said I'm fine, Danny. You're the one who's bleeding."

It was hard to tell where adrenaline left off and relief began. "Callie, if I tell you to get out, you need to get out. You could have been seriously hurt."

"Would you have left me?"

"Of course not, but—"

"It would have been three against one. You would have gotten the crap beaten out of you."

"Gee, thanks," he said dryly.

Her eyes widened in disbelief. "You're not seriously going to nurse wounded pride over this, are you?"

"No," he said softly. "No, I'm not. You're sure you're okay?" A beating he could take. Seeing her get hurt would have been far worse.

"*I'm* fine. Sit down, would you? Where's your first aid kit?"

He sat down on the top step and let her clean the cuts on his lip and his hand. The tips of her fingers guided his face upward to allow her better access as she dabbed at his injured mouth, and he tried not to stare at her lips, so close to his. They were nice lips, even though they were frowning at the moment. He had been tempted by them before, a few years ago when she had come home from LA to visit and he had realized she was far more woman than child now. His attraction to her had unsettled him and made him testy with her. Distant. He did not trust himself to get too close.

"Nice moves back there," he said, trying to lighten the mood. "Where did you learn them?"

She turned her attention to his hand. "You don't get mugged twice without deciding it's time to learn a little self-defense."

He laughed incredulously. "Paddling 101?"

She glanced up at him and grinned before focusing on his hand again. "It's all in the attitude, not the weapon."

God, he'd missed her.

"Should we call the cops?" she asked as she finished up with his hand. "I mean, those guys really could hurt somebody."

He forced his attention away from her fingertips on his skin and back to her words. "I'll take care of it. I know a patrolman who's really good at putting the fear of God into guys who like to get behind the wheel drunk."

"Really?"

"Not my first time with people like that."

"Oh." She wadded up the wrappers from the Band-Aids she had put on him. "Are you okay?"

He flexed his newly bandaged hand. "Right as rain, now."

Her voice was soft and hesitant, and the hardness he had seen in her so much since returning home was all but gone. "I meant—stuff like this. Does it take you back? To Elliot?"

Every time, he thought with a pang.

But he only squeezed her hand in his. "Let's not let what happened with those idiots ruin any more of our day, okay?" He frowned, a sudden thought occurring to him. "And maybe we shouldn't mention any of this to Liddy. She worries."

"Agreed." Callie stood up and reached for her purse, then looked at him as if she wanted to say something else.

"What?"

"Nothing." She started down the steps and toward her mother's car. A moment later, she turned around and came back. "Got plans for dinner?"

Something flickered inside him that he knew he ought to stifle, but he wasn't sure he could. His eyes settled briefly on her lips before he was able to force them upward again. He couldn't tell if she noticed. "Tonight?"

"Yes."

"I do now."

A slow smile spread across her face, and it was as if all the awkwardness between them had vanished. "Pick me up at seven." Then she got in her mother's car.

He watched her drive away, a dangerous glimmer of desire growing inside him. He was playing with fire here, and he would have to be careful.

The sound of footsteps on gravel made him turn his head.

Em stood with her empty lunch bag in her hand. She was staring at his bruised face. "Uh . . . did I miss something?"

His injured lip curved in a smile.

CHAPTER SIX

Callie checked her watch. Six forty. He would be here soon.

She stood before the mirror in her childhood bedroom, wondering for the umpteenth time if she ought to change. Maybe the shirt she had on was too low-cut, too clingy. Would Danny think she was trying to come on to him? Ridiculous, she told herself. She had worn this same shirt many times before and never worried about how she looked.

Then again, maybe it was too casual. But they were unlikely to go anywhere tonight that had a dress code, right? It was just an evening with two friends hanging out together.

She frowned at her reflection. The jeans had to go. Sliding the pants down her hips, she kicked them off and returned to her closet. She hadn't brought much with her from New York, and now she wished she had taken the time to pack more thoroughly. She pulled a summery skirt off a hanger and stepped into it. It was cute, breezy. A good choice for a warm evening. And if it showed off a fair amount of leg, well, she could live with that.

Fine, she thought, checking herself out in the mirror from every angle. Good enough. She had to stop stressing over this. She stepped into a pair of strappy heels and then paused, her eyes lighting on her hair. Maybe the bun was too formal, like she was trying too hard. She took the pins out and let her dark hair tumble down around her shoulders. That was better, wasn't it? Much more laid-back. Satisfied, she grabbed her purse from off the bed, and left the room, closing the door behind her.

A moment later she came back into the room and hastily put her hair back up again.

She couldn't remember the last time she had been this nervous before a night out. Not since she was a teenager, maybe. What was it about coming home that made her feel like the past was only days behind her and not years? The line between past and present seemed to be blurring. She only hoped it wasn't clouding her judgment.

"I could be back late, Mom, so don't wait up. Say hi to your friend for me." One of her mother's friend's from her church had made plans to dine in with Liddy tonight and watch movies. "If you need anything, I'll leave my cell phone turned on."

Her mother was on the couch with her leg propped up on pillows, reading a book. She glanced up as Callie descended the stairs, and she put the book down. "Oh, honey, you look lovely. Danny won't know what hit him."

"It's not a date, Mom."

Liddy shrugged and smiled, unconcerned. "Call it whatever you like. I just think it's nice you two are getting a chance to spend some time together, that's all. You are having fun, aren't you?"

Callie looked out the window. No sign of him yet. "Yes, it's good to see him," she replied absently, her mind elsewhere as she considered different options for dinner. Was the old diner still here? she wondered. It would be a shame if it had been torn down and turned into some strip mall or something. It had been a popular place for teenagers to hang out back when she had been one. There were a lot of memories there, and she was in the mood for a little nostalgia.

"As I recall, you used to have quite a thing for Danny, didn't you?"

"What?" Callie jerked her attention back to her mother. "I . . . What makes you think that?"

Liddy rolled her eyes. "Honey, please. I'm your mother. Of course I knew how you felt about him."

Her cheeks grew warm, but she pretended not to care. "I was a teenager, Mom. It was just a crush, nothing more."

"Maybe. But that was then, this is now. Would it really be such a bad thing if something happened between you two? Danny's a good man, and I know for a fact that there are other women in this town who would give their right arm for a chance to go out with him."

A flash of jealousy went through her. She turned back to the window to hide her feelings, hoping her mother hadn't noticed the telltale signs in her face. "You running a dating service now?"

"No, I just keep current on local gossip. Danny's considered quite the catch."

"Well, I'm not trying to catch him, so please don't try to force something that isn't going to happen."

"But—"

"Danny and I are just old friends, nothing more."

Her mother raised one eyebrow. "Are you trying to convince me or yourself?"

"I don't know what you mean," she said stiffly, knowing as she said it that she wasn't being completely honest.

"Oh, Callie," Liddy said softly, and a little sadly, too. "You're so bound and determined to keep your distance that you may wind up missing out on something wonderful. Don't cut off your nose just to spite your face."

Callie was silent. Her mother's words hit her harder than she expected, and she felt suddenly afraid. She wasn't sure of what.

Her mother continued, her voice almost hesitant. "Maybe it's my fault. Sometimes I worry that I'm the reason you left. You were angry, and maybe you had a right to be. But what scares me now is the thought that it's you who's getting hurt, sweetheart." She gave a little laugh, but it was one without much humor. "You're your mother's daughter, you know. Just as stubborn. And whether you believe it or not, I did what I thought was best concerning your father. Please don't let old hurts hold you back."

"I'm living the life I want."

"By leaving. Your father made the same choice. It's your choice to make, but please be sure you're making it for the right reasons."

Liddy sighed and leaned back into the couch cushions, rubbing her head with one hand as if she had developed a headache. "There's a lot you don't understand about your father, Callie. And maybe it is time I told you, but not tonight." She closed her eyes as the sound of a car turning into the driveway floated in through the window. "Danny's here. Go out and have a good time. And keep yourself open to possibilities, honey."

That was what her life was all about, wasn't it? Staying open to the possibilities that sprang up before her? Having tremendous life experiences, creating a life worth writing about . . . She felt an unsettling flicker of doubt, though. Without another word, she walked out the front door, closing it behind her.

The sense of anticipation she had been feeling earlier about the evening out with Danny seemed to have dissipated, and the heat of the dwindling day felt suddenly oppressive. She ought to have been pleased that her mother seemed finally to be coming around to Callie's point of view about her father, but the exchange with Liddy had left her feeling deflated instead. For a long time she had convinced herself that she was living the life she wanted— needed—and that she was happy with her choice. And there had been many moments along the way that she would not have traded for anything. But for the first time, she wondered what other moments she had missed out on in the process.

As she neared the end of the walkway, she looked up and saw Danny stepping out from his truck. For a second she forgot about the words she had exchanged with her mother.

Somehow he managed to pull off casual and striking at the same time. He would always be a jeans kind of man, but they certainly did look good on him. The cuffs of his ordinary white dress shirt had been rolled up, revealing tanned, muscled forearms, and as the corners of his mouth turned up in a warm smile of greeting, Callie felt her breath catch in her throat.

Who was she kidding? She would never be over him, not really.

His smile faded as she drew near enough for him to look into her eyes. "What's wrong?"

She tried to force a smile, but knew it wasn't very convincing. Instead of answering, she shrugged in dismissal and looked past him to his truck. "Ready to roll?"

Danny caught her arm, gently but firmly, as she started to brush past him. "Callie—"

She had to suppress a shiver when he touched her. After what her mother had said about Danny tonight, it was impossible for her not to imagine what it might be like if things were different between them. The nearness of him now made it hard to think clearly. "Let's just go," she pleaded, embarrassed that her voice wavered. "Please?"

After a long pause, during which she avoided his gaze, Danny released her arm. She reached for the door handle of the truck, but he beat her to it and opened it for her, a sweet, old-fashioned gesture that she secretly loved. As if tonight he saw her as a woman instead of just an old friend. She climbed into the truck and smoothed her skirt out as she waited for Danny to walk around to the driver's side door. Her heart had sped up when he held her arm, and it hadn't slowed back down yet.

Callie took a deep breath.

*

As he went around the back of his truck, Danny dug his nails into the palms of his hands in an effort to bring himself back to reality. She made looking beautiful seem so effortless, with casual locks of hair escaping from the pins in her hair and caressing her neck so invitingly, and her legs, bare in the summer heat . . .

He dug his fingernails in harder before he could finish that thought.

She was looking out her window when he got in the truck, her eyes on the front door of the house and her shoulders slumped. As he climbed in next to her, she quickly straightened her shoulders and put on a smile that he knew was a sham. Something was weighing on her. He had seen it in her face the moment their eyes met outside the house.

Danny turned the key in the ignition and put the vehicle in reverse. "Okay," he said, backing it up and then maneuvering it out onto the road. "We're going. Tell me what's wrong."

"Nothing," she insisted, turning the smile up a notch. "I'm fine."

"Bull. I know you, Callie."

A strange look crossed her face at his words. "Do you?" she returned softly.

He turned his eyes back to the road. "I may not know everything that's going on in your life now, but I know *you*. No matter how many tattoos you get."

He didn't have to look at her to know that she was still smiling, but now the smile was genuine. It pleased him to think he had made her feel at least a little bit better. "Mm," was all she said.

"Tell me."

She took some time, considering her words carefully. "I know I'm not the most dutiful daughter in the world, but I love my mom."

"I know you do. And you've been a great help to her these past few weeks."

"Maybe. I don't know. I know she loves me, too, but we've never been really close, you know? You'd have thought when Elliot died we would have turned to each other more, but—" There was a catch in her voice. "It didn't seem to work out that way. Sometimes it seems like we just tiptoe politely around each other."

Liddy had confided something similar to him once, in a moment of what she probably thought of as weakness. For two women who had trouble communicating with each other, they seemed to have a lot in common. He just wasn't sure that they realized it.

"Lately, though, things are more tense."

"Why?"

"Because . . . I want to find my father."

The circumstances under which Callie's father had left his family had always been vague in Danny's mind. Elliot hadn't seemed to know much about it, or at least he had professed not to care much about it. Liddy certainly hadn't shared any details with Danny, and it was hardly his place to pry.

"And your mom?"

"Doesn't think it's a good idea. She never has."

He glanced over at her and saw her biting her lip. "Why not?"

Callie shrugged, and there was a flicker of anger in her face. "She won't say. She won't say much of anything about him. I don't know if it was because of something she did, and she's too ashamed to tell me, or—" She hesitated.

"Or?"

"Or maybe . . . it was something about us? Elliot and me?"

"Ah, Callie," he said, distressed by the hurt he heard in her voice. "You were just kids. It wasn't your fault he left. I'm as sure of that as I am of anything. Sometimes married couples just aren't able to make it work."

"But if that's all it was, why won't she talk about it? Why wouldn't she leave me a piece of him to remember him by? I can barely picture his face now, you know that? It was like she tried to erase him. She had no right to take him away from me so completely like that. I feel like there's this whole other part of me that's just missing." She stopped abruptly, and clasped her hands together tightly in her lap. Her voice was clipped. "I'm sorry. I shouldn't have gone off like that. It's just been buried for a long time, I guess."

"I think you needed to say it."

She looked so forlorn, sitting there. Giving in to impulse, Danny reached out to take her hand in his own and squeeze it. She curled her fingers around his, and after a moment of hesitation, she leaned toward him to rest her head on his shoulder. Tentatively, at first, as if she wasn't sure if it was all right. He squeezed her hand again, still held in his, and she relaxed against him. It was difficult for him to keep his attention on the road.

"I have this one memory," she said, so softly he almost missed it. "My dad and me, walking somewhere. A park, maybe. I must have been very young, four or five. He held my hand for a while, and then he put me on his shoulders. I felt like a giant. He laughed at something; I don't remember what." Her voice was wistful. "He had such a nice laugh. I remember feeling happy then, like everything was just perfect." Then she gave a sad little excuse for a chuckle. "Well, what does a five-year-old know about the world, anyway?"

No wonder coming home was hard for her. "Sometimes our parents don't exactly live up to our childhood expectations, do they?"

"No, I suppose not." Then he felt her raise her head from his shoulder. "Danny?" she asked hesitantly.

"Yes?"

She seemed to think better of whatever her question would have been. "Forget it," she said. "None of my business."

"No, what?"

"I just was wondering . . . what happened with your parents? In all the years we've known each other, I've never heard you say a word about them."

It was a long time before he answered her. "That's because they weren't worth mentioning."

"I'm sorry," she said quickly. "Like I said, none of my business."

"It's all right," he said. His voice was curt, but he hoped she knew it had nothing to do with her. He had been eight years old when he came to live with his grandfather in this town, and Miles had thought it best not to share much family history with friends and neighbors. Danny had followed his example. He had told Elliot some things, trusting his friend to keep them to himself, and Elliot had not let him down. Judging from the look on Callie's face, her brother hadn't even told *her*. "I envied you and Elliot when we were kids, you know that? I envied what you had with your mom."

Callie was silent.

"I know you don't remember much about your dad," he continued, his eyes on the road and his voice flat. "I never even met mine. Don't know anything about him. My mom was a junkie. She had lots of boyfriends—or maybe johns, I don't know. It wasn't exactly a model home life." Home. The word hardly applied to any of the places they had lived. They had never stayed in one place long enough for any of them to ever feel like a home anyway, and his mother had left a string of angry landlords and unpaid rent behind her as she and Danny skipped from city to city.

Flashes of memory came to him that he thought he had long ago buried. Winters spent without heat or electricity, telltale rat droppings in corners of apartments that should have been condemned long ago . . .

Callie's voice brought him back to the present. "She abused you?"

"I went hungry a lot of the time, but I preferred the days when she forgot she had a son living under the same roof as her."

"Oh, Danny," Callie breathed in shock. "I had no idea. I'm so sorry."

"It's okay," he said, clearing his throat. "That was a long time ago."

"Did . . . did she die?"

"I don't know. My grandfather got me out of there when I was eight. Some place back east. St. Louis, maybe, I don't know. Haven't seen or heard from her since."

"Your grandfather got custody?"

"Well . . . sort of. He tried jumping through the right hoops first, but never got far. So finally he just came right out and asked her what it would take for her to give me up. She named a price. He emptied out his bank accounts."

He heard Callie's sharp intake of breath beside him.

"And then he brought me home." Danny didn't trust himself to speak any more about what had happened back then. The old man had saved him from hell on earth and had given him the first real safe place he had known. Words could only express so much anyway.

"And you let me go on about *my* problems. You should have just told me to button it."

He grinned then and glanced over at her. She looked chagrined, sitting there beside him. "Hey, don't look so worried," he told her with a nudge. "It had a happy ending after all." Then his smile faded, and he turned his face back to the road before she could notice the sadness that he thought might have shown in his eyes.

"Did Elliot know?"

"A little."

She was silent for a long time. "Your grandfather used to scare me a little when I was a kid," she said finally. "He was so stern and everything. But right now I think he might be my hero."

"Yeah," he said gruffly. "Mine too."

He could feel her eyes on him, and her concern. It wasn't exactly the way he had imagined the evening going. "Enough heavy stuff for one night," he said decisively. "Did you have some place in mind for dinner tonight, or should I pick?"

"Well . . . there was this one place I used to go to hang out with friends back when I was in school. I don't even know if it's still there. A La Mode?"

"Yeah, it's still there. Man, I haven't been there in years. What made you think of that place?"

She shrugged, a little more cheer in her eyes than before. "Reliving my youth, I guess."

"Exactly what kind of youthful experiences are we talking about here? I seem to remember A La Mode as being hookup central for teenagers."

She laughed. "I'll never tell."

The pall over her seemed to have lifted. "You prefer to leave it up to my imagination?"

"Hmm. When you put it that way . . ."

There was a devilish gleam in her eyes as she shot him a sidelong glance. He felt the same rush of heat that had hit him earlier that day when she had asked him to dinner. There was little point in lying to himself about his growing attraction to her. The trouble was that he wasn't sure what to do about it. Although he had never considered himself a player, he had dated more than a few women before and had never had any problem figuring out what to do or say around them. Callie was different.

Could she tell? It was probably better if she couldn't. She had made it very clear that she would not be sticking around. The thought occurred to him that maybe he could change her mind and make her want to stay, and he despised himself for thinking it. Manipulation had never appealed to him.

But what was one evening, after all? He could enjoy the nearness of her without crossing the line.

He hoped.

From the outside, A La Mode appeared to be unchanged. It was a replica of an old fifties diner with fitting images of icons like Marilyn Monroe and James Dean painted on its sides as murals.

"Do you think the jukebox is still here?" Callie asked as they stepped out of the truck.

"Only one way to find out."

It was there, in all its lit-up glory, and the strains of Chuck Berry greeted them as they walked through the front door. Old movie posters and Hollywood-esque memorabilia decorated the walls, and the waitresses wore poodle skirts. It didn't seem to be crawling with teenagers tonight, but there were a few there, making noise and trying to impress members of the opposite sex.

"Oh, wow," Callie breathed. "This takes me back. Senior prom, homecoming . . ." She smiled. "Jennifer and her long list of crushes. And Tony. Oh, yes, Tony."

It was ridiculous to feel jealousy over the memory of one of her high school boyfriends, but it was there nonetheless. "I probably don't want to dig into your sordid past and ask who Tony is, do I?" he asked, trying to keep his tone light.

She pretended to be offended. "Sordid? Tony was a perfect gentleman. Well, almost."

"So we're here to relive your past conquests then?"

"There was more angst than conquest."

A grey-haired waitress dressed in a bright pink poodle skirt and wearing a nametag that said "Shirley" on it seated them at a back booth, away from some of the more boisterous teenagers.

"I don't think *she* was here before, but everything else looks the same." Callie was clearly delighted. "Isn't it great? Tacky, but great."

Danny was more distracted by Callie than by the décor in the diner. The dark clouds around her earlier had completely lifted, and her eyes sparkled like sunlight on water. "Yeah."

"Where else could you go and find Elvis salt-and-pepper shakers?" She held them up for him to better appreciate them.

"Good point. I'm completely won over now."

The truth was that he was having a few vivid memories of his own about this place. Fond ones. Girls, football celebrations, double dates with Elliot. The feeling of anticipation when the girl he liked smiled shyly back at him.

Sitting across from Callie now, he felt as if he were back in high school again. He thought his palms might even be sweaty.

They ordered cheeseburgers, the house specialty. The burgers were as large as he remembered, nearly too big to fit a person's mouth around them, and they tasted as good as they used to, too.

"So what about you?" Callie asked, looking at him over her hamburger as she prepared to take a bite. "Any conquests to brag about?"

"Conquests? No. But there were good times."

"Is this where you would take your dates?"

Danny shrugged and tried not to stare at her mouth. "Some of them."

"Followed by a drive up to Cutter's Lookout, no doubt," she said knowingly.

He nearly choked on his burger. "And how do you know about Cutter's Lookout?"

"You're kidding, right? Everyone who was ever a teenager in this town knows about Cutter's Lookout."

"You went there," he said, confirming more than asking. It was the make-out capital of the county. There was suddenly a sour taste in his mouth that had not come from his burger.

Callie put her burger down on her plate. "No," she admitted, unaware of the relief that flooded him. "I was invited a couple of times, but not by anyone I cared to go with." She looked at him speculatively, a small smile playing at her lips. Those lips were driving him to distraction. "Did you ever go?"

He raised his gaze from her lips to her eyes. "No," he said finally. Was it his imagination or did she look a little pleased by his answer? "I guess there wasn't anyone I cared enough to go with either."

*

She should not be asking him these kinds of questions. They just seemed to spill naturally from her. And maybe she was crazy, but it seemed as though he was paying an awful lot of attention to her mouth. Each time his eyes lingered on her lips, she felt a little thrill of anticipation go down her spine.

She let her eyes drop briefly to *his* mouth. As a teenager, she had often fantasized about kissing it. She thought maybe one reason why she had let Tony kiss her—once, only once—was because he had looked a little like Danny.

But there had been no spark because he *wasn't* Danny, and so the kiss was not repeated.

Their waitress, Shirley, appeared just then, startling Callie back to the present. The older woman placed a large chocolate shake and two straws on the table.

"Oh—we didn't order this," Callie said quickly.

"On the house, honey. A sweet treat for a sweet couple." Shirley beamed at them both, clearly pleased with herself.

Warmth flooded her cheeks as she gave a Danny a quick glance. "We're not—"

"Thank you," Danny said, interrupting her and smiling back at the waitress. "Very much."

"My word, the way you two look at each other takes me back. My Henry wasn't quite the looker that you are, young man," she said with a wistful look into the distance and a motherly pat on Danny's shoulder, "but he hung the moon as far as I was concerned. Married forty-three years now, too."

"Congratulations."

"Enjoy it, kids," the woman said, winking before leaving.

Callie wondered if she meant the chocolate shake or the feelings she thought were between them. Or the way she thought they looked at each other. She felt herself blush again, and she raised her eyebrows at Danny. "You just capture the hearts of waitresses everywhere, don't you?"

He raised his own eyebrows in return, the corners of his mouth twitching.

"You shouldn't have let her leave that here," she said with a nod toward the chocolate shake.

"No?"

"It was under false pretenses."

He put one straw into the shake and held the other one out to her. "You really want to spoil her fun?"

After a moment, she took the straw from him and sank it deep into the milkshake, sending some of the whipped cream topping over the edge of the frosted glass. Without thinking, she ran one finger up the side of the glass to catch the excess and bring it to her mouth. She glanced up to see Danny watching her.

"What?" she asked, suspecting she knew full well already but enjoying the hint of color that came to his cheeks. It was about time someone besides her did the blushing around here. She licked the whipped cream off of her finger very deliberately, feeling a little bit wicked as she did so. Until today, she hadn't known Danny was capable of blushing.

"Nothing." His voice held a faint note of strain, and he glanced away.

She put her straw to her lips and took a long pull on it. "Mmm. They don't make milkshakes like this in New York. Aren't you going to have some more?"

After a moment, Danny leaned in for a sip on his own straw, a move that brought their faces very close to each other. "I wouldn't want to disappoint Shirley."

It was fun, this teasing back and forth. Callie held his eyes with hers for as long as she could as they sipped, but this close to him, it was hard to do. She was the first one to look away this time. Her knee brushed against his under the table, and she shivered in reaction.

"Too much milkshake?" he asked, misinterpreting the shiver.

Callie rubbed her bare arms and played along, nodding. "Guess so."

"Yeah. Don't think I can handle much more, either." He signaled their waitress for the check, leaving Callie to wonder if there was more than one layer of meaning in his words.

Shirley delivered the check and placed her hands on her ample hips. "Had enough? Looks like there's still a little shake left in there. You want me to put it in a to-go cup for you?"

"No," Danny said, handing her some money, "but thank you. Everything was as good as we remembered."

"Ah. Locals, then? Or maybe used to be. Let me guess: you two used to come here in high school, right?"

"Guilty," Callie agreed.

The woman pursed her lips and considered them with shrewd eyes through her horned-rim glasses. "High school sweethearts?"

Callie's nervousness resurfaced. Funny how she kept floating between self-conscious and bold. "Oh, uh—no. I was a few years behind him in school." She glanced at Danny and thought he looked like he was enjoying her discomfiture. There was mischief in his face.

"Really? So how did you meet?"

"Go ahead, honey. Tell her." A slow grin curved Danny's lips, and when Shirley favored him with a glance, Callie took the opportunity to shoot him a dirty look.

"I don't think so—" she demurred.

"Oh, but I love a good how-we-met story," the waitress pleaded, clasping her hands together in anticipation. "Come on. Humor an old lady."

Danny's grin grew wider. "Yeah, *sweetheart*, come on."

Fine. If he wanted to play, then Callie could play, too. "If you insist, darling."

"Oh, absolutely."

Shirley sighed, her eyes turning dreamy. "Was it love at first sight?"

"Nah, not really. Well, for him it was. We passed each other on the street and he used some clichéd line about me looking familiar." She shrugged and gave him a smile full of saccharine sweetness. "I wasn't really all that interested, to tell you the truth, but the poor guy just kept following me around like a lost little puppy until I finally took pity on him and agreed to go out with him. I mean, I hate to see a man beg."

Unseen by Shirley, Danny clutched one hand to his heart as if wounded.

"So we went out, and he was so nervous that he kept forgetting my name."

Callie reached out to pat him on the hand. "Poor thing! You were just tripping all over yourself, weren't you?"

He caught her hand in his and brought it to his lips. "Can you blame me?"

As his lips brushed the skin of her hand, Callie forgot what she had been about to say next. She was saved by Shirley.

"Aww. And he's still just as lovestruck! So he won you over, huh?"

Her hand was still in his, and he didn't seem to be in any particular hurry to give it back. "Yes. Yes, he did," Callie finished lamely.

"And the rest is history. I don't see a ring on that finger, though." Shirley picked up their half-empty mug. "Best not to dawdle in that department, young man."

"No, ma'am."

"Well, you kids have fun tonight. The night is young, and so are you. Have a good one." She nodded cheerfully as she left, humming the tune to an old love song that Callie couldn't quite place.

"Lost little puppy, huh?"

"Yep. You should have seen yourself. Totally besotted."

"*Besotted*? Spoken like a true writer. Thanks for not giving me a facial tic or a unibrow, by the way."

"I was working up to that part of the story."

"Ah," he said sympathetically. "Too bad it got cut short. Lucky for my poor, battered ego, though." Standing up from the table, he offered her his arm, still in character. "You heard the lady. The night is young. I don't have a curfew. Do you?"

Aware that Shirley could still see them, Callie took his arm with a coy smile.

"Not last time I checked. What did you have in mind?"

He grinned. "Soothing my wounded pride."

CHAPTER SEVEN

"So the first one to get all of their balls in the holes wins, right?"

Callie was looking up at him with a look of intense concentration, as if she was taking mental notes. She held a cue stick in one hand as if she wasn't sure which end of it was supposed to point up.

"Pretty much. But they're called pockets, not holes, and you can't touch the balls directly with your cue stick."

She frowned. "How am I supposed to get them to go anywhere then?"

Danny held up the white cue ball. "You hit this with your cue stick, and then it hits the ball of your choice. Ideally, at least." He demonstrated for her, placing the ball on the table and striking it smoothly to send it careening toward a striped one. The striped ball sank into the corner pocket.

"Okay. Let me try." Callie bent over the table and tried to mimic Danny's motion. The cue ball went sailing off the table. "Son of a—"

Danny caught it before it got very far.

"Sorry," she said, frowning.

"Hey, it happens to everybody when they're first learning," he said generously, but he was grinning as he said it.

"Uh huh. How's that wounded pride doing?"

"Better now, thank you."

The pool hall was dimly lit, but there was enough light for him to clearly see the beginning of a smile on her lips. She turned to lean back against the pool table, and the light silhouetted the feminine lines and curves of her body, the length of her legs beneath her short skirt. The faint strains of blues music drifted through the faintly smoky air, and she drummed the fingers of one hand on the wooden rail of the table in time to the music's beat. She made an inviting picture, and he couldn't resist drawing closer.

"I could give you a few pointers," he said, moving around the table to stand directly in front of her. He reached for the cue stick in her hands. "If you're interested."

"You're going to turn me into a master player?"

"I'm good, but I'm not that good."

She gave a burst of indignant laughter and threatened to hit him with her free hand. He put one arm up in front of his face in mock defense. "Fine, maestro. Bestow some of your grand expertise upon me."

"All right." Danny gestured behind her. "Turn around."

She looked startled. "What?"

"Turn around. Close to the table, feet apart." After giving him a wary look, she followed his direction. "Then lean in." He wrapped his arms around her to place one of her hands down on the surface of the table and the other around the butt of the cue stick. Her back was against his chest, and her ear close to his mouth. A tendril of dark hair that had worked its way loose from the knot she had wound it up in brushed against his cheek like a caress, and he felt heat growing inside him again.

"Is pool by any chance an excuse men use to get their hands on a woman?" she asked over her shoulder.

"It's the reason most of us play, actually."

"Ah." Her tone was light, but it seemed to him as if she was holding her breath. "What do I do next?"

He guided her hand into placing the narrow end of the stick in the crease between the thumb and index finger of her other hand. "Now you aim for the center of the cue ball."

"That's the white one, right?"

"Right." Her hand moved beneath his, sliding the stick back and forth, and then striking the ball. It rolled cleanly forward before hitting another ball and sending it in the general direction of the far pocket.

She turned her head slightly, her mouth inches from his. "Better?"

He tried not to stare at her lips. "Much."

Dear God above, her skin smelled incredible.

"So . . . now what?" she asked softly, her eyes dropping to his mouth.

Was he imagining things, or was she giving him the green light? His body was suddenly full of new tension. He could almost feel her lips against his then, and his ability to think clearly abandoned him.

Her lips parted slightly as he focused his attention on them, and he wondered if she knew what he was imagining.

A shout of victory from another pool table broke the trance Danny seemed to be in, and he looked away. He was thinking crazy thoughts. Foolish thoughts. It had been a bad idea to put his arms around Callie like he had. Had he really thought he would be immune? He straightened and took a step back from her.

"Now," he managed finally, his pulse erratic, "we rack 'em."

He put the balls in the rack at one end of the table and then put the cue ball in its place at the other end. Callie remained silent. Glancing up at her, he couldn't read her face well enough to be sure what she was feeling, but he thought a shadow flickered across it. Disappointment? Or was that wishful thinking on his part?

"Lady's choice," Danny offered amiably, trying to recover the playful mood from earlier. "Do you want to break, or shall I? I mean—take the first shot."

"You can go." She reached for her beer and took a sip, her face still a mystery to him.

He took aim with his cue stick and sent the balls scattering across the table. None went into the pockets, and he grimaced.

He was not exactly focusing well at the moment. "Your shot. You pick, solids or stripes."

"Okay." She set her beer down and picked up her cue stick again. "So are we playing for anything?"

"You mean stakes?" he asked, a little incredulously.

"Yeah."

"Are you serious? You've had a sum total of one lesson."

She shrugged. "But you seem a little off your game there, pal. I'm feeling kind of lucky. Besides, we're just having fun here."

Of course she meant pool, but his mind was still on how close he had come to kissing her. She would not be looking to start something now, not when she was so hell-bent on leaving town again. They were having fun together, that was all, and he would do well to remember it. If he kissed her, though, he didn't think he would be able to stop at fun. He would do well to remember that, too.

Danny rubbed chalk on the end of his cue stick, forcing his attention back to the game at hand. "What kind of stakes did you have in mind? Bragging rights? Next round of beers, maybe?"

"Boring."

"Then what do you suggest?"

She leaned forward against the table, and a hint of creamy cleavage distracted him. "Hmm. For now, let's just say the loser is in the winner's debt." The faintest suggestion of a smile played upon her lips. "For a favor to be named at a later date."

She was killing him, and she probably had no idea of it. "That could be dangerous."

Her eyes flashed. "That's what makes it fun."

"You're sure? Don't think I'll let you out of it, if you change your mind later."

"I won't." She held her hand out.

"Deal." He took her hand in his to shake it. Such a casual touch between them shouldn't have affected him, but it did.

"All right, then. I'll take stripes." Callie leaned over the table and placed her hands perfectly before drawing her arm back and striking the cue ball dead center. It sailed into a solid red ball, which then struck a striped one and sent it rolling directly into a side pocket.

Danny's eyes widened.

Callie took the chalk from his hand and applied it to the tip of her cue stick. "Corner pocket," she said matter-of-factly, lining up her shot. A moment later another ball rolled merrily where she directed it.

A slow, rueful smile spread across Danny's face. "You little— I've been hustled, haven't I?"

"What? I told you I was feeling lucky." She circled around the table and chose her next target. With apparent ease, she banked the next ball off the wall of the table and sent it into the middle pocket on the opposite side.

"Remind me never to play poker with you."

Callie sank another ball. "No promises."

He started to laugh. "'The first one to get all of their balls in the holes wins, right?' How do you keep a straight face?"

"Years of practice. It's a handy way of making a little cash when you're on the road." She finished playing the table. "Eight ball in the side pocket." The ball followed suit, just as she predicted. "And there you have it."

Shaking his head, Danny wryly applauded her performance. "Well played."

"Thanks." Callie laid her cue stick on the table and put one hand on her hip as she turned to him. "*You're* not going to try to get out of the bet, are you?"

"Can't. You know where I live."

She grinned.

"So," he asked, with an exaggerated wince, "what's this favor I'm going to have to owe you?"

She leaned over to begin retrieving the balls from the collection chamber of the table, a position that drew attention to the shortness of her skirt and the length of her legs beneath it. A pair of men one table over paused in the middle of their game to take notice, and Danny deliberately stepped in the way to obscure their view, frowning darkly at them.

Callie seemed not to notice any of it. "Don't worry. It won't be anything you'll mind losing."

Yes, she was killing him.

*

Callie felt awfully giddy for a woman who had only nursed one beer that night. It could hardly be the drink going to her head. The air felt thick around her. It was either the heat of the summer air, or it was something about the way Danny's arms felt around her waist during their impromptu pool lesson. She would be lying to herself if she said it was anything but the latter. His voice, so low in her ear as he guided her in striking the ball, had made her legs feel weak beneath her, and his breath on her cheek had nearly been her undoing.

Any other man she knew would have kissed her when she was that close, looking back at him the way she had. Why hadn't he? She thought he had wanted to, but maybe she was mistaken. Maybe she was allowing wishful thinking to affect her judgment.

She watched him play the table, his attention seemingly focused entirely on the game. He was totally at ease as he moved. Casual. His movements were so relaxed that each shot seemed as natural to him as breathing. That was not the way he had been with her earlier. No, she thought, she had not mistaken the tension in his body when his arms had been around her and her mouth had been so close to his. It was the response of a man to the nearness of a woman that he wanted but would not let himself have.

She wondered why he wouldn't. There was no one else that she was aware of in his life. And her mother, she thought wryly, seemed to be keeping pretty current on Danny's love life. Then again, her mother's accident may have left her out of the social loop lately. She thought back to the other night they had been out together, and an unpleasant possibility came to mind.

"So . . ."

He glanced up from where he was leaning over the table in preparation of his next shot. Once again, Callie noticed the way his jeans fit him so well. How could one man be built so perfectly in so many places? "What?"

"I'm curious. Did you ever call that waitress?"

"Waitress?" he repeated, looking blank. "What waitress?"

"You know. The one from the other night." Callie took another small sip from her beer and tried to sound nonchalant. She pretended an intense interest in her fingernails as she spoke. "The one who wrote her number on the check."

Danny made the shot, his face turned away from her. He made a sound like a cough that might have been covering up a laugh. "Oh. You mean the one you said was 'tacky'?"

"That's the one."

"Why do you ask?"

He was going to make her drag it out of him, wasn't he? Pride should have stopped her, but her need to know overruled it. "Like I said. Just curious."

"Really?"

"Yes, really," she said, a little irritably. "Unless it's some great secret, of course."

He shrugged. "No."

"No, it's not a secret, or no, you didn't call her?"

"Yes."

"I'm going to hit you in a minute."

This time he laughed for sure. He turned to face her and leaned back against the pool table, one hand resting on the tip of his cue stick. "There's no need for violence," he said, his eyes twinkling at her. "I'll talk."

His smile could have melted polar ice caps. He seemed to be able to resist her, but she wasn't sure how much longer she could resist him. "I'm listening."

"No, I didn't call her."

Relief flooded her. She hoped it didn't show on her face. "Why not? Not your type?"

The twinkle in his eyes faded. "No." Pushing himself off of the table, he turned back to his game. "Not really."

She was an inch away from asking him what his type was, but it occurred to her that she ought to know that about him already. Danny wasn't one for drama or high-maintenance in a woman. He would want someone down to earth, like he was. Someone who shared his passion for simple pleasures outdoors, someone who loved small towns.

Someone who loved family and wanted to put down roots.

Not someone who moved on when roots threatened to hold her back.

She felt that same strange flicker of anxiety that she had felt earlier that evening when her mother had warned her about what she might be giving up. She did her best to shake it off, but a kind of melancholy took its place, just as strange and unsettling. It would be so much easier if she could be that person her mother, and maybe Danny, wanted her to be. It seemed like it should be enough to make her happy. She wasn't sure why it wasn't.

That was why he hadn't kissed her, she thought distantly, her eyes on the pool table but not really seeing it. He might be attracted to her—and she believed maybe he was—but he would not want to start something with her that they couldn't finish. He was not the kind of man to indulge in a casual romance.

She smiled sadly to herself. She wouldn't like him so much if he were.

It was fun, this flirtation between them. And it felt like sparks flew off her skin whenever he touched her. But she would be making a mistake to try to make something more out of it. He clearly knew it, and she ought to make peace with it herself.

"What are you thinking about?"

Startled from her thoughts, Callie glanced up to see Danny watching her. He had cleared the table at some point, and she was embarrassed to realize that she had no idea how long she might have been staring off into space. She looked away. "Oh, just thinking about something my mom said tonight."

"You okay?"

"Yeah." She smiled with more cheer than she felt. "Just figuring a few things out, I guess."

"About you and your mom?"

It was easier to focus on that side of it with him. "Maybe that's part of it."

"I know you guys butt heads sometimes, but you're here now, when she needed you, and she'd do the same for you in a heartbeat. You two are so much alike, you know that? But maybe it's easier for me to see that since I'm on the outside looking in."

"Maybe."

He set his cue stick back in its place and stood in front of her, his hands in the pockets of his jeans. "You know what you said earlier, about you feeling like you weren't close to your mom?"

"Yes."

"Liddy said almost the same exact thing to me once, about the two of you. A few years ago, after the last time you left. She was afraid you were going to drift even further apart than you already were, and she hated the fact that you were so far away."

"I know," Callie acknowledged, her eyes downcast.

His voice softened. "But she was so proud of you, too, Callie."

Her head shot up again. "She was?"

"Yes. It took guts to do what you did, to be on your own and take chances that way. You knew what you wanted, and you went after it. Not many people could do what you did, and she was proud that you could make your own choices without needing anyone else's approval. She bragged to people about some of the things you did. Some of the things you wrote about."

Her voice trembled with emotion. "Really? Why didn't she ever tell me?"

He leaned against the wall beside her and nudged her with one shoulder. "You're kidding, right? Because she's just like you. I never met two more stubborn women in my life."

Callie smiled weakly, struggling to maintain her composure.

"Seriously," Danny said, the warmth of his body so close to hers comforting and reassuring. "I think maybe she was afraid that if she gave you her blessing, you'd take it and run with it, and you'd disappear into the farthest corners of the world where she would never see you again. Like your father, maybe. I think she was afraid of not being part of your life anymore."

Callie wiped her eyes quickly as they grew wet. "Well, that's just ridiculous."

"Maybe you should tell her that. Somebody's got to go first, you know. Might as well be you."

"This counseling a side business of yours?"

"More of a hobby."

"You're not bad," she admitted.

He gave her another companionable nudge. "Liddy's leg doing okay?"

"Doctor says she's healing like a pro," Callie told him, grateful for a change of topic before her emotions could overwhelm her. "She gets around really well with her walker. She's itching to get back to work, too, I can tell. Mom's never been one to stay idle for long."

He made a noncommittal sound of agreement or acknowledgement and reached for his drink. "Still planning on leaving town?" he asked, taking a sip and not looking at her.

"Yeah," she said quietly, not looking at him either.

"Back to New York, or someplace new?"

"Got a few loose ends to tie up in New York. After that . . . I'm not sure."

"I see." There was an awkward pause before he spoke again. "You must have racked up a long list of pen pals, what with all the places you've lived," he said in what she knew was an attempt to speak lightly.

She shrugged with a half-smile. "Not as many as you'd think. Most of the folks I spend time with are just 'passing through,' like me."

They remained shoulder-to-shoulder, silent for a long while. "Sounds lonely," Danny said finally, the words soft and hard to hear.

Lonely. She had never thought of it that way before. To her it had just seemed practical not to form too many attachments. Why let herself get close to people she might never see again? There would be fewer goodbyes that way, and fewer disappointments.

She felt an urge to protest his words, but could think of nothing to say.

His cell phone rang then, and she was left alone with troubling thoughts as he glanced at the caller's number and stepped away to answer it.

*

"What happened?" Danny listened to the voice on the other end. It belonged to a neighbor, someone to whom his grandfather had been a good friend years ago and who was now returning the favor. "Is he all right . . . ? Tell him I'll be home soon. I'm sorry . . . I'll be there as soon as I can. Thanks for staying with him."

He ended the call, pausing to collect himself before he turned around and went back to Callie. She had enough on her mind right now, and the last thing she needed was for him to unload his own problems on her.

He closed his eyes and took a deep breath, quelling the ache inside him. It was a terrible thing to feel so helpless to help the one person he loved best in the world, the person to whom he owed so much. Few people knew the truth about his grandfather's failing health, and he would do his best to keep it that way for as long as possible, out of respect for his grandfather's wishes.

But it was getting harder.

"I—" He stopped and tried again, keeping his expression neutral. "I have to cut the evening short. I'm sorry."

Callie's frowned, concerned. "What's wrong?"

"It's just . . . nothing. I'll take you home." He forced a smile. "We'll have a rematch some other time."

"Danny—"

He shook his head firmly. "Don't worry about it."

She let the matter drop, but clearly did not believe that it was nothing. The ride back to her mother's house was a silent one until they pulled into the driveway. It had been an amazing night, one he thought he would never forget no matter how far away Callie's life might take her, and he didn't want it to end on a sour note, at least not for her.

"I had a good time," he said, turning his head to smile at her in the darkness of the cab of his truck. "Even though you did wipe the floor with me."

Light from the moon illuminated her answering smile. "I had a good time, too.

Thanks for everything."

If this had been a date, he would have leaned in to kiss her now. If ever there was a right moment, this was it. But if he kissed her, there would be no going back to the way things were before and no way to pretend it hadn't happened. And she would still be leaving. She might stay a little longer, but she would still leave in the end. And if she came back somewhere down the line, they would be unable to slip into the familiar roles of friends with that kiss hanging between them. Which meant she might not come back to him at all. One kiss could end up costing him more than he was willing to pay.

"Well," she said finally, opening the passenger's side door, "good night, then."

"Good night."

He ought to have left it at that, but instead he leaned toward her before she could close the door. "So did you give any thought to going out on the river? It sounds like we may not get many more chances to do it before you leave."

"That would be fun."

"Saturday?"

She nodded in the moonlight, but shadows prevented him from seeing her face. "Saturday."

"Pick you up at nine?"

"No, I'll meet you there."

"Okay. See you then."

He watched her walk up to her front door and go inside.

Saturday. He should be distancing himself from her, not making excuses to see her again.

Once again, he was playing with fire.

*

There's a lot to be said for having friends and family around you. When life throws you something unexpected, you don't have to face it all by yourself, alone. There are shared memories, shared joys and heartaches . . . connections. If you are lucky enough to find yourself blessed with such people, you can count yourself rich many times over. To ask for more would be crazy. And ungrateful.

Why, oh, why do I still feel like something's missing?

What am I still looking for?

Callie closed her notebook and stared out her bedroom window at the night.

CHAPTER EIGHT

Callie had packed much too lightly when she left New York. She was lucky that her mother had not emptied the old bureau in Callie's former room and donated all of her old clothes to charity. Granted, much of what remained was no longer in style, and a few things didn't fit Callie exactly the way they used to, but there were still plenty of t-shirts and tank tops that were serviceable—

She reached in and pulled out some black fabric.

—and one black bikini. It was very plain and ordinary, but it hardly made sense to go out and spend money on a new swimsuit just for one day on the river. Besides, she planned to wear a t-shirt over it anyway, so it didn't really matter what it looked like.

She tried it on in front of the mirror, just to make sure it still fit, and it did. Maybe a bit too well. She was a little curvier now than she had been at sixteen, and the suit showed it. Self-conscious, she pulled on the first t-shirt she could find, one bearing the name of a rock band she barely remembered anymore. Better, she decided, examining her reflection. Less attractive, but better for that same reason. More conservative. She was finding it hard enough to be around Danny and not want to get closer to him, and if he felt anything like she did, than it would be wiser not to show much skin. Skin made a person think about reckless things, like what it might feel like to touch it.

She had found a tube of sunscreen in the medicine cabinet earlier, and now she rubbed it on her legs and arms, her mind drifting back again to Danny. It was probably a bad idea, this day in the sun they were planning. If she were smart, she would have called up and canceled. On the surface it sounded innocent enough, but she would be alone with him, and it was hard enough for her to keep her head on straight when they were in the presence of other people. Alone with him, anything could happen.

An image flickered into her mind before she could stop it, her fingers sliding up his back, his mouth on her neck. She closed her eyes and allowed herself to indulge in the fantasy for a moment. She had wanted him since high school, and clearly, time had not changed things. If anything, her years away from him had only made it clear that other men did not affect her the way he did.

Would it really be so wrong to give in, just a little? Just to allow herself something to hold on to and remember down the road?

Callie opened her eyes, suddenly ashamed. Giving in would be selfish. It would be bliss, she was sure, but then it would turn to regret. Not just for her, but for Danny. Because she would still leave, she knew that, and it would hurt him. She might want to stay, but a part of her wouldn't let her do that, and she wasn't sure why. But she was sure that she would never forgive herself if she hurt Danny.

She finished dressing and went downstairs, stepping softly. There was no sign that her mother was up yet, so Callie moved about the kitchen quietly, forcing herself to eat something for breakfast because she was more tense than hungry. Danny had said nothing about food, but they would likely be out for more than a little while. A picnic lunch might not be out of place. Nothing fancy, she thought, opening the refrigerator door and rifling through the contents. Some fruit, cheese . . . maybe some crackers. Her fingers hovered over a little plastic basket of strawberries, and another image came into her head, one of her holding a ripe berry to Danny's lips to feed him.

She left the berries untouched in the fridge.

A few minutes later, she left the kitchen with a brown paper sack of snack foods thrown hastily together and a bottle of water. She glanced at her watch: time to go. But she hesitated a moment longer with a look down the hall toward the closed door of her mother's bedroom. They had been avoiding each other since their last conversation. She started to take a step toward the door, intending to knock, and then stopped. This was not the time. Danny was expecting her, and a conversation like the one she hoped to have with her mother would likely not be a quick one.

Sighing, she turned to go to the front door. A piece of paper was taped to it, a bit of quick handwritten scrawl across it. Drawing closer, she recognized it as her mother's writing:

Callie,

Dinner at 6:00.

We need to talk.

A prickle went up Callie's spine. It had to have something to do with her father.

Would it be the answers she had been wanting, or would that door be shut in her face again? Once more, she was tempted to go and knock on her mother's door, but she was afraid to push her luck. If her mother really was about to finally open up to her about Callie's father, the wrong word at the wrong time could wreck things, and who knew when she would get this chance again? It would be wiser to wait.

Reaching into her purse, she grabbed a pen and scribbled a brief response, her hand shaking slightly.

I'll see you at six.

She drove with the car window down, hoping the fresh air would clear her head. It was warm already, even at this early hour, but blessedly free of the humidity she had grown accustomed to on the East Coast. She would miss that when she left. She would miss a lot of things.

For what might have been at least the hundredth time since she had been home, she considered the possibility of what might happen if she stayed. She had barely entertained the thought before a panicky feeling that might have been akin to claustrophobia began rising up inside. She had never been able to explain it before, and she couldn't now. Instead, she buried it again and turned her thoughts elsewhere.

The roads were hardly crowded, but there was more traffic than she had expected at this time of day. Many of the vehicles she saw were towing boats or bicycles, evidence of plans for the day. Several cars seemed to hold families, kids bouncing around in the back seat in anticipation of the day ahead. For the first time in a long time, she felt a touch of wistfulness at the sight.

By the time Callie reached Danny's rafting outfitter, she was a mass of confusion and jumbled feelings. Things had been so clear to her back in New York. Now she felt as if she had no idea what she really wanted. It was driving her crazy. She didn't need these complications.

Danny's truck was parked out front. A pair of oars was visible in the truck bed along with a small raft, just large enough for two people.

Go, a little voice inside Callie's head pleaded with her. Just turn around and leave. It could be a grave mistake for her to go with him today, considering how she felt about him. She was asking for trouble.

But it was one of the last chances she would have to see him before she left, she told herself with a pang of sadness. Soon enough she would be thousands of miles away from him, and who knew when she would see him again? She didn't belong here with him, not in the long run, but she could have the here and now as long as she didn't let herself get too close. It was just one day, after all.

Then he appeared, walking around the corner from the back of the building, and she had no choice but to stay now. His face wore a distracted look, as if he was deep in thought, and she wondered if it had anything to do with her. He glanced up, seeing her car, and a warm smile spread across his face. Her breathing sped up.

He ambled casually toward her car, the very picture of a man relaxed, and she thought he must not have been feeling anything quite like she was feeling if he could approach her so easily. Taking a deep breath, she opened her car door and stepped out. "Morning."

"Morning." He adjusted the weathered baseball cap on his head. "Glad you made it. I wasn't sure if you'd be used to such early hours, after life in the big city."

He was teasing her, she knew. She forced the same lightness into her own voice. "Ha. You have no idea what city life is like, buddy. I keep hours that would drop you."

"Sure, you talk big, but let's see how you hold up. Ready?"

Callie grabbed her few things from off the front seat. "Lead the way."

*

The ride in the truck was a quiet one.

Danny thought Callie's cheerfulness seemed stiff, as if she was doing her best to hide somber thoughts beneath it. He supposed he was doing much the same thing, trying to act natural when he felt anything but. Today's outing may have been a bad idea since each time he saw her it grew harder and harder for him to maintain the line between friendship and something more. He had considered canceling, but could not bring himself to do it.

You're a fool, he thought to himself. *It will only make it harder to say goodbye to her when she leaves again.*

Danny turned his attention to the road again.

He knew this river as well as he knew himself, and today he planned to take Callie to a spot that he doubted many other people had ever seen. It was alongside an offshoot of the river that was challenging to navigate but worth the trouble when the end was reached. He had discovered it one day when he had been craving an escape from tourists and was willing to endure a bit of a struggle in order to venture off the beaten path.

Today would be the first time he had taken another person there. He wondered if Callie would see the same beauty in it that he did.

He turned the truck down a dirt road and followed it to its end, little more than a small clearing a stone's throw from the water's edge. "We'll put in here," he said, getting out of the truck. Without a word, Callie helped him get the raft out from the back of the truck and carry it to the river. She let him put the food she had brought into a cooler he had prepared, and watched him stow the few other things they had with them as compactly as possible.

"Is there room for *us*?" she asked doubtfully, eyeing the small raft.

"Just try to think of it as cozy, not crowded."

"You're the expert."

They pushed the raft out into the water before climbing aboard. The water was cool, refreshing in the growing heat of the morning. Danny smelled the scent of sunscreen on Callie's skin as he settled behind her in the raft, and he marveled again at how pale she was. "When's the last time you spent an entire day outdoors, Callie?"

She considered his question. "Probably the last time I was on the water with you," she said finally.

Seated behind her as he was, he couldn't see her face, but he thought there was a note of something in her voice that he couldn't quite place. Nostalgia, maybe? Maybe he only wanted it to be.

He remembered the last time they had gone rafting together. She had just graduated from high school, and their trip was meant to be celebratory. Callie had been full of laughter that day, and full of mischief. She had begged him to hit the roughest patches of whitewater, alternating between cajoling and making barbs about his manhood to try to shame him into doing what she wanted. It had been the most fun he'd had in a long time, and it might have been the first time Danny had realized that his best friend's little sister was growing up. It was certainly the first time he remembered feeling any kind of pangs of self-consciousness around her.

She spoke as if reading his thoughts. "So, are we hitting the rapids today?"

"Not today."

"What are we doing, then?"

He used an oar to push them out into the current. "Exploring."

"Going where no man has gone before, eh?"

"Well . . . not many."

He let the current carry them most of the way, relaxing and reveling in the stillness of their surroundings. This far from town, there were no sounds of cars to break the silence. The only sounds to be heard were the occasional cry of a bird and the sounds of the river as it coursed forward. Did she like it, too? he wondered. Or did she miss the sounds of city bustle?

Her head tilted slightly, as if she was listening, too. A bird of prey swooped down to pluck a fish from the water, and Callie straightened, exclaiming and pointing. Danny smiled inwardly, pleased to see her enjoying herself.

A few minutes later, they veered down the narrow offshoot for which he had been aiming. This part required careful navigation due to sharp rocks protruding from the water, but rafting was like breathing to him, and he got them through it with no trouble. He headed the raft to the shoreline a short distance downstream where the water flowed into a small, still pool that was beside a sandy strip of beach. It was surrounded by steep hillsides and trees on all sides, and it was peaceful in its seclusion.

"Well," Danny said, letting their gentle momentum carry the raft a few inches up onto the beach. "What do you think?"

"Oh, Danny, it's beautiful," she breathed, and when she voiced her approval he felt tension he hadn't realized he had been carrying relax. "How did you ever find this place?"

"Just followed my instincts, I guess."

"Do you bring any of your customers here?"

"No. Never."

"Good," she said, sounding relieved as well as pleased. Stepping carefully from the raft, she waded in ankle deep water toward the shore and kicked off her shoes. After making sure the raft wasn't going anywhere, Danny grabbed their things and followed her.

"Too early to eat," he noted, spreading out a large blanket and putting the rest of their things on top of it. "But not to swim. It's warming up already. Care to join me?" He drew his shirt up over his head and tossed it aside along with his baseball cap.

"Maybe in a minute," she answered, lowering her eyes. "You go ahead."

"Suit yourself." He waded back into the water, out where it was deepest, and dove beneath it.

*

Callie sat onto the blanket, trying hard not to watch Danny as he surfaced and then dove again. Her eyes betrayed her, though, and they refused to look away. His body was lean and hard everywhere, and tanned by countless hours in the sun. Droplets of water trickled down his chest and stomach, following the contours of the muscles there. Her mouth grew dry, and she reached blindly for her bottle of water. Did his skin feel as smooth as it looked? She closed her eyes and drank deeply.

The sun climbed further overhead. Its heat beat down on her, and she thought how inviting the water looked, particularly with Danny in it. Don't do it, her inner voice warned her frantically, but she slid her shorts down over her long legs and kicked them off, then took hold of the t-shirt she had sworn she was going to leave on and pulled it off over her head, leaving only her swimsuit underneath.

Standing up, she walked slowly toward the water's edge. Danny surfaced again, wiping water from his face with his hands and then letting them fall to his sides as he caught sight of her. She was not bold enough to make eye contact with him, but she continued into the water without pause, willing herself not to blush under his scrutiny. The coolness of the water was a shock against her bare skin, but she went in deeper, needing the cover it offered from his eyes. It was only deep enough to come up just past her waist, though, so she dived beneath the surface as Danny had done moments earlier.

When she came up again, it was with her back deliberately to him. She ran her fingers over her hair to wring out some of the water there. "Very refreshing," she said over her shoulder, but her voice sounded strained even to her.

"Yes, it is."

She heard ripples move across the water, and she knew he was moving toward her. She wanted him to, and yet she panicked at the thought of what he might do when he reached her. She lost whatever nerve she'd had that had compelled her to enter the water in the first place, and she began to wade back toward the shore. "I know it's early, but I could do with something to eat. You want something?"

*

Yes, Danny thought, watching her step out of the water. *You.*
"All right," was all he said.

Her body was lithe and lean, and he suspected it would haunt his dreams from now on. He thought he had been in trouble before, but now he knew he was lost. There was no way it was humanly possible for him to make it through this day without touching her.

His eyes were drawn to the small of her back. "So you weren't making it up."

"Making what up?" she asked as she rummaged through the cooler.

"Your tattoo."

She paused. "Oh. That." She reached for her t-shirt and put it on, covering the small black design from view.

He followed her out of the water. "What is it?"

"It's Japanese." She seemed intently focused on the contents of the cooler and didn't look up as he approached.

"Does it mean something?" he asked, settling down onto the blanket beside her.

"Loosely translated, it means something like 'free spirit,'" she answered, shifting her position to put a little more space between them. "Do you disapprove?"

She was as much on edge as he was, he realized. "No," he said softly. "It suits you."

"Thank you," she said, sounding surprised. She held out an apple, conjuring up images in his head of Eve in the Garden of Eden. "Fruit?"

He deliberately let his fingers touch hers as he took it from her. Her cheeks turned pink, and he didn't think it was from the heat of the day. "Can I take a look at it?"

"Take a look at what?"

A slow grin curved his mouth. Yes, she was nervous. It made him want to touch her all the more, she, the hardened woman of the city. "Your tattoo."

Callie hesitated. "Oh . . . Okay."

She turned her back to him and lifted the hem of her t-shirt. He had only meant to look at it, but he couldn't resist the opportunity to touch her. Danny reached out to trace the lines and curves of the symbol, and Callie tensed beneath his hand. Her skin was as soft as silk, and it took all of his willpower to draw his hand away. "Beautiful."

"Thank you." She let the shirt drop down again to cover her skin from view.

"When did you get it?"

"A couple of years ago. Before New York."

He bit into the apple. "What was the occasion?"

Callie didn't answer him right away. A shadow flickered over her face. "There was a guy," she said finally. "We got close for a while, but he wanted more than I could give him, and things went south. I got the tattoo as a sort of reminder not to make the same mistake again."

The apple lost its sweetness. "Which was?"

"Getting involved with someone who wanted me to be something I wasn't."

Her words had the effect of ice water being thrown on him. "I see," he said, trying to keep any trace of bitterness from his voice. He threw the rest of his apple into the underbrush, any appetite he might have had gone.

What did you expect? he thought darkly at himself as the silence stretched awkwardly between them. She had been perfectly clear from the start about what she wanted from life, and she was reminding him of that now. It wasn't her fault if he had let his feelings get the better of him.

"Hot out," Callie said with a shaky smile. "Think I'll go cool off again."

She got to her feet and returned to the water, stripping her t-shirt off again at the last minute and wading in.

He watched her go, wanting her as much as ever and cursing himself for a fool. He had done this to himself, let himself get close to her again only to know that he was going to have to say goodbye. Like the man she had spoken of moments ago, he had allowed himself to want too much.

Danny lay back on the blanket and closed his eyes, trying to recapture his self-control.

*

Callie stayed in the water for a long time, hoping to cool off her emotions as much as her body. She loved the way he teased her, the way he had touched her. His fingers on her back had nearly been her downfall. Then she had brought them both back to earth, and she had seen the disappointment in his eyes.

Her throat hurt, as if her words to him had choked her. She had done the last thing she had ever wanted to do, and that was to hurt him. Did he think she didn't want him? Surely not. He must know how important he was to her. But then, how could he, if she had never told him? All she had done was leave town and break off all contact with him for four years. It had been because she had been crippled by her feelings for him, but he had no way of knowing that.

She turned to look at him where he lay on the blanket and felt the lump in her throat grow.

She didn't want to leave him. Why couldn't she stay? Why couldn't she just ignore that nagging fear that always pushed her to keep moving? Tears threatened to spill, and she blinked them back.

What scared her the most, though, was the thought that she wouldn't be able to keep that inner voice smothered permanently. It was too persistent. She would have to find a way to silence it for good before she could risk getting involved with Danny and hurting him more deeply.

At the moment, he lay so still with his eyes closed that he might be sleeping. Wading silently through the water, Callie stepped onto the beach and let her eyes roam over him. It was unnerving how much she wanted him. No other man had affected her this way before, and she guessed no other man ever would.

With silent footfalls, she crept to the blanket and knelt down beside him, careful not to disturb him. His eyes remained closed, so maybe he really was asleep. She allowed herself to watch him a few moments longer, and then she covered her face with her hands and sighed into them. It was torture to be so close to him and not be able to touch him. Praying for self-restraint, she let her hands fall away from her face, and one of them brushed against Danny's hand.

His hand curled around hers before she could pull away, and she drew her breath in sharply, startled that he had not been asleep after all. His eyes remained closed, but he caressed her hand with his fingers very gently, sending sparks through her with that simple touch.

"I missed you." The words slipped from her in a whisper before she could stop them. She *had* missed him. For four years, she had missed him, even though she had seldom allowed herself to think about him. It had taken her far too long to say the words to him.

He turned his head and opened his eyes to look at her, still massaging her fingers between his. "Did you?"

She couldn't speak. She could only nod.

His eyes burned into hers. "I missed you, too."

She should have pulled her hand free of his by now, but instead she let him pull her slowly down to him. "Danny—" she started, trying to muster up one final scrap of self-control.

Cupping her head in his other hand, he cut her off by bringing her mouth to his. She put her free hand on his chest to balance herself and felt the muscles in his torso tense beneath her touch. It was a heady feeling, knowing that he wanted her the same way she wanted him.

His lips were every bit as amazing as she had imagined they would be. A part of her was stunned to realize that it was Danny McCutcheon's hand she felt at her waist, Danny's breath on her skin, Danny's lips on hers. He had been all she thought about when she was barely into womanhood, and so now it almost seemed more likely that this was all a dream instead of reality.

He whispered her name against her mouth.

She kissed him again, allowing her hand to slide over his bronzed skin like she had fantasized about doing for years, and he let out a guttural sound. Hesitating, she started to draw her hand away, but he put it back where it had been and rolled over until she was beneath him, careful not to crush her beneath the weight of his body. His lips left hers and traveled over her neck.

Callie closed her eyes, knowing she should stop him, stop both of them, but completely lacking the will to do so. He tasted the skin at the base of her throat while one hand slid along the full length of her arm and finally entwined itself with hers. Callie's free hand slipped down along his spine. His muscles were taut beneath her hand, and she knew he was struggling with himself, trying to rein in his desire so as not to overwhelm her.

He was being so careful with her, and she was not doing the same for him. It was that thought that finally enabled her to speak.

"This is . . . this is a bad idea," she managed to say, hating the words even as she said them. Her voice faltered. "Danny?"

He pulled back from her slightly, leaving her feeling bereft, and touched her cheek. "I know," he said quietly.

"I'm sorry. I'm so sorry." The tears that had threatened earlier filled her eyes again.

"Me, too." For a moment, he buried his face against her neck as if breathing her in, and she didn't ever want to leave.

She wrapped her arms around him and hugged him tightly, knowing she should let him go but struggling to do it.

"Ah, Callie. Don't cry."

"I'm not," she said as the first tear traveled down her face.

He sat up, taking her with him, and cradled her against himself. His breath in her ear sounded ragged, and she felt his heart racing in his chest where her cheek touched his skin.

"I'm sorry," she repeated. "I want to, Danny, I do. But I can't. Please try to understand."

She felt his fingers stroke her hair, but he didn't say anything. Was he angry with her? Maybe he had a right to be after all of her indecisiveness. With a heavy heart, she drew back from him and searched his face.

If he was angry, he hid it well. All she saw on his face was regret. "It was my fault," he said. "I knew better than to—" Breaking off his words, he cupped her face between his hands, and for a moment she thought he might kiss her again. She half-wished he would. And finally he did, but it was a chaste kiss on her forehead, the kiss of a friend instead of a lover. "Come on. We should go."

Callie nodded, and he helped her up from the blanket before bending back down to pack things back up into the cooler.

She watched him silently, afraid she might be making the biggest mistake of her life.

CHAPTER NINE

Neither of them said anything the whole way back to the truck, and once they got into the cab of the pick-up, Callie kept her face turned toward the side window until they reached the outfitter again.

Danny bit back the words that he really wanted to say, namely that nothing in his entire life had felt less like a mistake than kissing her, and did she really not feel that way, too? Words like that would probably just make her run away faster.

Idiot, he cursed himself. He had known better than to cross that line with her, had known all along that she was just passing through. Only a fool would get involved with someone that he knew would leave. Or a masochist. He liked to think that he was neither.

So he had agreed to call it a mistake and let it go at that, or try to. And he would step back and watch her leave, he thought with a pang, because it was clearly what she wanted. Better for him to make a clean break quickly instead of trying to drag things out.

But the pang grew sharper. He stifled it and pulled the truck into the parking lot beside Callie's car. "So," he said, clearing his throat. "Heat of the moment. Heat of the sun, maybe, affecting our judgment."

She nodded, still not looking at him. He was disappointed by her quick agreement, but not exactly surprised. She swung the passenger's side door open. "I'll see you," she said stiffly over her shoulder.

"Yeah." And that was the only thing he could think of to say. It was just as well. He couldn't have faked nonchalance for much longer, and he wasn't sure she was buying it anyway.

He watched her get into her car, and then he quickly put his truck in reverse, feeling a need to get out of there before she did. Turned out, he wasn't up to watching her leave after all.

*

Callie's drive home was blurred by tears. She finally pulled over to the side of the road, afraid that she was a danger to other drivers this way. It was impossible to think clearly beyond the fact that she might have just screwed up the best friendship she had ever had. And it had been stupid to think that a few memories of her visit here with Danny would be of comfort to her down the road. Instead, it would be hell on earth to think about it, knowing now exactly what it was that she couldn't have.

You foolish, foolish girl, she berated herself.

She couldn't go home yet. It was far too early, and her mother would suspect something had happened. If the shortness of their rafting trip weren't enough to clue her in, Callie's face would do the rest. She wiped at her tears with one hand and took a few deep breaths. When she thought her emotions were reasonably under control again, she pulled the car back onto the road.

She didn't know where she was going yet, and the thought made her laugh, albeit without humor. Hadn't she lived her whole life not knowing where she was going? Why should today be any different?

By the time she got back into town, she still had no clear idea of where she was headed, but somehow her car wound up near the park that she remembered walking through with her dad years ago. She couldn't remember the last time she had been here. Surely she had been here once or twice after he had left, hadn't she? But it was all vague in her mind.

Getting out of the car, she wandered aimlessly onto a wide, grassy knoll and down to a footpath. Nothing looked familiar to her until she reached a large stone fountain. Coins covered the bottom, and Callie had a vague recollection of tossing a few pennies in with her father. Was it possible, she wondered as she ran her fingers through the water, that the very coins they had thrown in were still there? Unlikely, she supposed, feeling a wave of grief that surprised her.

A terrible tiredness hit her, far beyond skin deep. Everything seemed to be wrong somehow, and she couldn't escape the feeling that it had all started going wrong right here, with her father. All of her adventures on the road, all of her wild and wonderful exploits, had been a vain attempt to prove that she was all right, that his leaving hadn't really hurt her. But she thought now that maybe she had never really gotten over it after all.

Just ahead of her was a patch of grass beneath the overhanging limbs of a huge tree, shaded and serene. She sank down onto it and leaned back against the tree trunk, grateful for the support it lent her.

She was so tired.

*

Callie opened the front door slowly. It was close to six o'clock now. She had spent most of the day just sitting in the park, trying to shut out thoughts of Danny and failing miserably. Her next move was easy to predict. This was the part where she packed up her things and left town because the walls were closing in.

But this was Danny. She had walked away once before and regretted it. If she walked away again, she wasn't at all sure that she would be able to come back. It might be too difficult to mend things now as it was. They could hardly pretend the kiss hadn't happened.

"Callie?"

Her mother's voice drifted to her from the kitchen. Callie took a deep breath and willed herself to appear calm. "I'm home."

"Dinner's just about ready. Did you have a good time?"

"Yeah, sure. Look, Mom, I'm going to take a quick shower, if that's okay. I'll only be a minute."

Her mother poked her head out of the kitchen, supporting herself quite ably with one crutch. "Are you all right? You don't sound like yourself."

"Just tired." Callie avoided her mother's questioning look and climbed the stairs. Once in her room, she peeled off her clothes and stepped into the shower, turning the water on full blast and scrubbing herself roughly. The urge to run was strong inside of her right now. This was not the restlessness that had kept her moving from place to place the last several years. This was fear, plain and simple. Fear of not having Danny in her life anymore. Fear that she had hurt him today by giving in to a selfish urge, and fear that she could hurt him even worse if she stayed and continued to behave so recklessly.

She shut the water off and rubbed herself dry with a towel, still none too gentle. She stared at her reflection in the mirror, her pale skin pink from the harshness of her rubbing, and wondered why she seemed to be her own worst enemy. But her mother was waiting downstairs, so there was no time to analyze herself now. She threw on her nearest clean clothes and went to meet her mother.

The table was set with a simple meal, one with familiar classics whose scents triggered childhood memories. Rosemary mingled with chicken. It had been one of Callie's favorites growing up, and she suspected that was why Liddy prepared it tonight. "Wow," Callie murmured, sitting down at the table. "You made all this with a bum leg? You shouldn't have gone to all that trouble. We could have ordered in."

"Not tonight." Liddy sat at the head of the table, and now she unfolded her napkin and laid it across her lap. "Besides, a body can only sit so long before going stir crazy. And I do love a challenge."

Callie raised her glass in salute before taking a sip of water. "That you do."

They ate in silence for a few minutes, seldom making eye contact. Callie began to wonder if her mother had changed her mind about the purpose of tonight's meal. It wasn't until their plates were nearly empty that Liddy finally spoke again.

"So. You want to find your father."

At her mother's words, Callie froze with her fork halfway to her mouth.

"I've been doing a lot of hard thinking about this, honey." Liddy cleared her throat and tried again. "I'll be honest with you. This is very difficult for me to talk about. I loved your dad a lot, and when he left us, it nearly broke me. I had expected happily ever after, but I got my heart handed to me on a plate instead. It hurt a lot, Callie, and I was angry for a very long time. I honestly thought the best thing for you and Elliot was to cut out any painful reminders of your dad—and I still think you're better off without him—but it's very possible that my anger and hurt feelings clouded my judgment."

Callie put her fork down and held her breath, afraid that if she interrupted her mother, she would stop right there and go no further.

"Please believe me, Callie, that I have never in my life wanted to do anything to hurt you." Liddy's voice shook slightly before she got it under control again. "And if it was a mistake to keep the details about your father locked away from you, then I'm sorry. Truly, I am."

Tentatively, Callie reached out her hand to her mother.

Liddy took a deep breath and held her daughter's hand tightly in her own. "I'm afraid that if you go looking for him, hon, that you won't like what you'll find. I think it will only hurt you. But maybe it's what needs to happen so you can move forward. So . . ." She reached into her pocket to pull out a folded piece of paper, which she then held out.

With her hand shaking slightly, Callie took the paper and unfolded it to read it.

There was a name, a phone number, and an address on it in Chicago. James Sorenson. Her father's name.

"I had to reach out to a couple of his old friends. He moves around a lot, kind of like you. If—when," Liddy corrected herself, "you go to see him, don't call first. Just go."

"But—"

"If you let him know you're coming, sweetheart, he may be gone before you get there."

The words were a bit of shock.

Liddy smiled sadly. "Baby girl, he's always been good at leaving. He couldn't face you back then to tell you goodbye. Don't expect him to be a better man now."

Callie blinked in surprise and then stared down at the name on the paper. "Why did he leave, Mom? Was it something we did?"

"Don't ever think that. It was him, not you. It was always him. Oh, honey," Liddy said, worry in her voice as she reached out to cup Callie's cheek in her hand. "Are you sure you want to do this?"

All her life she had wanted to do this. She still did, although there was a knot in her stomach now. "I have to see him."

"I had a feeling you'd say that." Liddy sighed. "When will you go?"

She wanted to go right this second. "Well . . . you're getting around pretty well now. I don't think you really need me to be here anymore, do you?"

"I'll be fine," her mother said quietly, but there was grief in her voice.

Callie pushed her chair back from the table and went to kneel beside her mother's chair. "Mom," she said earnestly, looking up into Liddy's face. "I'm not Dad, okay? I'm not walking out. I'm in your life for good, and I'm afraid you're stuck with me."

It had been a long time since the two of them had hugged each other. Callie felt a little rusty and awkward as she put her arms around her mother, realizing how much it must have cost her to say what she had said tonight, but Liddy didn't seem to mind. She returned her daughter's hug without hesitation, stroking Callie's hair as she had done when Callie was just a child. "And you're stuck with me, kiddo. Go do what you need to do, but always know that home is here for you. Anytime."

"Thank you."

Her mother sniffed and sat back in her chair, wiping her own eyes. "Bah. Far too much emotion for one night. Look at us! I won't tell anyone if you won't."

Callie smiled at her mom. Maybe Danny had been right. Maybe they really were two of a kind. But her smile faltered as she thought of him.

Her mother seemed to have thought of him, too. "So, you'll want to tell Danny goodbye before you jet off after your father, won't you?"

She knew her face had betrayed her when she saw Liddy's brow furrow. "I . . ."

"What's wrong? You two didn't have a fight today, did you?"

"No. Not exactly." But she couldn't look her mother in the eyes.

"Well, something happened."

"I . . . I screwed up, Mom. I crossed a line with Danny today, and there's no way to uncross it."

Liddy looked faintly alarmed. "What exactly did you do, Callie?"

"I kissed him," Callie said heavily.

"Oh." Her mother gave a little laugh of relief. "So what's wrong with that? Sounds to me like this should be good news, not bad. Good grief, Callie. You had me worried there for a minute."

"Mom! This isn't a joke."

"Who's joking? I think it's high time you two got around to a little action."

Callie's eyes widened and she had to reach out and catch the arm of her mother's chair to keep herself from falling over. "Mom!"

"What?"

"Could you not be so . . . blunt?"

Her mother rolled her eyes. "Life's too short to dance around the truth. I would think that you, of all people, would be in favor of a little frankness."

Callie sank back into her own chair and leaned back, covering her eyes with one hand. "Not when it's my mother discussing my love life."

"Fine. I'll try to censor myself around you. But I still don't see why you think what happened with Danny today was a mistake. You like him, don't you?"

"I like him a lot, Mom. And he likes me. That's the problem."

"That's a problem?" her mom asked incredulously.

"It was for you and Dad, wasn't it?" Callie returned, dropping her hand and looking her mother in the face. Liddy had been the one to suggest frankness, after all. "I mean, I'm sorry for bringing it up, but you said yourself that it devastated you when he left, because you cared about him so much. I would think you would understand better than most."

"Danny's not like your father, Callie."

"I know that, but I'm afraid I am."

"That's ridiculous."

"He left. I left."

"Yes, but you came back," Liddy pointed out.

"But for how long? I already want to run, Mom. Everything inside me is screaming to get out of Dodge."

"I think that's because you're scared, honey."

"Yes, I'm scared. I'm scared I'm going to hurt Danny more than I already have."

"You would never hurt Danny like that."

"Do you think Dad thought he would hurt you?" Callie asked softly.

Her mother was silent.

"What if I'm just like him? I'm not sure why I can never seem to stay in one place for long, but sometimes I think it's because I'm trying to understand him. And all I really know about him is that he left us, so maybe that's why I'm so good at leaving, too."

"Then maybe you're right that it's time to go see him, Callie." Liddy shook her head and sighed. "Maybe then you'll be able to see yourself the way I see you."

"Maybe," Callie agreed, sounding unconvincing even to herself.

"Well, whatever you do about your father, honey, don't leave without seeing Danny first, no matter how awkward you might feel. It hurt him the last time you left, you know, and it would hurt him again. He's got enough to deal with right now." Then Liddy bit her lip, as if she had said too much.

Callie frowned. "What do you mean?"

"I shouldn't have said anything. He hasn't told many people, and it's his business to share, not mine."

"Told many people what?" Her mother hesitated, and Callie repeated her question more insistently. "Told many people about *what*, Mom?" Her heart sped up. "He's not sick or anything, is he?"

"Danny's not sick, Callie. His grandfather is."

"Sick with what?"

Her mom hesitated again.

"Sick with *what*, Mom? Tell me."

"He has early Alzheimer's."

"Alzheimer's?" Callie sank back onto her knees. Her mind went back to the other night in Danny's truck and to the way he had spoken of his beloved grandfather. "Oh, no . . ."

"It's in the early stages still, but Miles is a proud man, and the news came as quite a blow to him. He hasn't wanted to tell anybody about it yet, so Danny's been doing the best he can to honor his wishes and take care of him himself, but he's had to enlist the help of a neighbor lately."

"Is it . . . progressing quickly?"

"I'm not sure. I know Miles is on medication, but Danny doesn't like to talk about it much. I think it's too hard for him. He loves that old man, you know."

"Yes," Callie said softly. "I know." Abruptly, she stood up. "Mom, I have to go. Just leave everything on the table, and I'll clean it up when I get back, okay? But I've got to go."

Her mother nodded, and Callie knew she didn't have to ask where Callie was going.

*

Evening was not far off. Danny stepped out onto the front porch of the well-weathered house he shared with his grandfather and leaned against the railing to stare out at the trees surrounding the borders of the property. There was nothing extraordinary or fancy about the place, but he still saw it the way he had seen it as a boy the first time he had come up the driveway with Miles, and that was as a paradise. Set back from a winding road outside of town, it was quiet and still, the complete opposite of the jarring noise and chaos that had always surrounded his mother. Here he was safe. Here he was loved.

There was a lump in his throat tonight. He had come home from his disastrous day on the river with Callie to find that his grandfather, so calm and grounded normally, had had a meltdown because he had forgotten the name of his deceased wife's favorite flower, a daisy. Their neighbor, Mrs. Grady, who had been looking in on him regularly, had been unable to calm him.

Then Danny had come home, and things had gotten worse.

He breathed the clean, clear air in deeply and tried to ignore the feeling that his world was slowly falling apart.

The noise of a car's tires on the graveled driveway made him turn his head. Recognizing the car and the driver behind the wheel, he straightened in surprise. Of all the visitors he might have gotten, he had not expected to see Callie tonight. Not after the way they'd left things.

She stepped out of the car and into the twilight, and he thought he had never seen anything in his entire life that he wanted more. For a moment, he remembered the taste of her mouth, and the way her fingers had curled tightly around his, and it was all he could do to keep his hands in his jeans pockets instead of grabbing her as she slowly climbed the steps of the porch.

She stopped at the tops of the steps. "Hi," she said uncertainly.

He nodded his head in response, speechless and still astonished to see her there.

"Oh, Danny." Her voice was soft and sad. "I'm so sorry about your grandfather."

"Ah," he said flatly, looking away. "Your mom told you."

"I don't think she meant to, but I'm glad she did." Whatever surge of boldness that had prompted her to come here tonight seemed to desert her. She crossed to the other side of the porch as if needing to put more space between them. "How is he doing?"

"Most days aren't too bad, not yet. But he forgot something today that was important to him." Danny leaned back against the railing again for support, feeling empty and tired. He hadn't intended to tell Callie any of this since she would be leaving soon. There was nothing she could have done anyway, but the words spilled out of him, and it was something of a relief to be able to share them with somebody. "It scared him. A lot."

She took a hesitant step toward him. "I'm so sorry. This must be horrible for you."

Watching someone he loved go through this and feeling so completely helpless to help him was torture, especially after everything his grandfather had done to help him. Danny cleared his throat, keeping his face averted from Callie's. To have her so close right now was both comforting and painful, and if she came much closer, he wasn't sure what might happen. He had already proven today that he lacked self-control around her, and even now he could feel the muscles in his body tensing. "It scares me, too. There was a moment today when he looked at me and he didn't know me, Callie. He didn't know me."

He stopped, unable to say more. The moment had passed with his grandfather seemingly unaware of the slip in his memory, but Danny had been deeply shaken to think that there might come a time when Miles wouldn't remember him at all.

The touch of Callie's hand on his shoulder finally made him turn his head to look at her. Tentatively, she slid her arms around his neck and pulled him closer to hug him, and his arms automatically wrapped around her in return.

Careful, he cautioned himself, but his body didn't seem to be listening.

After what had happened between them this morning and the way she had fled from him after that, he tried not to hold her too tightly, but she felt too good not to hold close. The warmth and softness of her were soothing and comforting after the unsettling afternoon with his grandfather. Turning his face into her hair, he breathed in the sweet scent of her.

Careful, he thought again, and for a moment he was afraid he had said it out loud when she drew back from him. But she didn't go far. She looked at him with wide, troubled eyes, but her arms remained around his neck. It took all his willpower not to lean in and kiss her when she looked at him like that. "Danny," she whispered, and his grip around her waist tightened.

Hesitantly, as if she was warring with herself, Callie tilted her head to kiss him so lightly that he almost thought he had imagined it. Then her mouth opened against his, and he lost himself in the feel of her.

*

She had not come here intending to do this. Truthfully, she hadn't come here with much in the way of a plan at all. All she had known was that she had to see him, to see if he was okay. They had been friends long before they had been anything else, and as his friend, she needed to be here.

The kiss that had begun so gently turned into something else entirely. As Danny's arms tightened even more around her waist, her own arms pulled him nearer, and her fingers buried themselves deep in his hair. She felt his body tense against hers, and together they stumbled back against the porch railing. Gone was the restraint he had shown this morning, and right now Callie didn't care if he ever got it back. She should, she knew she should. But she didn't.

She tore her mouth away from his long enough to draw in a breath of air, and in the absence of her lips, his mouth found her throat. Tilting her head back, she closed her eyes and reveled in the feel of him. His mouth was hot on her skin, his hands everywhere. Without pausing, he lifted her onto the edge of the railing so she could wrap her legs around his waist and pull him closer. It still didn't feel close enough.

His fingers dug into her hips, and she drew her breath in sharply, surprised at the desire it triggered in her. Danny drew back as if startled. "Sorry," he told her, his breath ragged. "Did I hurt you?"

She shook her head, unable to speak.

But he seemed to think otherwise. Instead of resuming his onslaught of her senses, he rested his forehead against hers and closed his eyes, his chest rising and falling rapidly. Callie put her palm there and felt his heartbeat racing, nearly as fast as her own. "Ah, Callie," he whispered. "What are we doing?"

"I don't know," she whispered back.

"I think you know how I feel about you. And I think you feel pretty much the same way about me, too." He straightened and traced the features of her face with the fingers of one hand as if memorizing them. "But I don't want to start something we can't finish."

Callie gave a shaky little laugh. "I think it's a little late for that." And it was exactly what she had not wanted to happen.

"Then stay. You don't have to leave. Stay with me and see what this turns into."

"I don't know if I can."

"Why not?"

She dropped her gaze, ashamed. "What if I'm just like him, Danny?"

He furrowed his brow. "Just like who?"

"Dad." She thought of the hurt in her mother's eyes tonight, still there years after her husband had walked out on her.

"You aren't your father, Callie. You aren't bound by his mistakes."

Though it was the last thing she really wanted to do, Callie gently pushed Danny away from her enough that she could slide off the railing and back onto her feet, softening the gesture by twining her fingers through his. "Easy to say, but I need to figure it out for myself."

"How? By leaving again?"

"I'm going to go see him, Danny. Mom got his address. He's in Chicago."

He took a step back from her, and their hands separated. "So you're going to Chicago?"

"Yes."

"When?"

"As soon as I can."

"And after you find him? Then what?"

"I don't know," she said helplessly. "I don't know what I'll find there."

She could see in his face that he didn't think she would be coming back to Rockford Falls. Or to him. She hoped she would, but she was afraid to make a promise she might not be able to keep. As it was, she had already gone back on her resolve not to repeat this morning's mistake.

They stood in silence for a while as the air grew darker around them and the first stars appeared overhead. "I should go," Callie said finally, awkwardly. Danny didn't respond, so she turned to go down the porch steps, each step heavier than the last. She had hurt him again anyway, in spite of her intention not to do so. Just as she reached her car, his voice stopped her.

"Callie?"

She turned to look back at him.

"I hope you find what you're looking for."

Me too, she thought pensively.

As she drove away from the house, she glanced in the rearview mirror, but Danny was gone.

*

Let her go, Danny thought, letting the front door close behind him as he reentered the house. *You go your way and let her go hers*. Anything else would just be inviting needless grief. He had enough of that to deal with right now without looking for more.

As he came into the living room, the sound of quiet singing broke his train of thought. It was his grandfather's voice, soft and low, and coming from down the hall. Walking with silent footfalls so as not to startle Miles, Danny approached the door of the back bedroom. It was ajar, and through the crack he could see his grandfather sitting on the edge of his bed with a picture frame in his hands. The frame was a familiar one, and Danny knew it held a smiling portrait of his grandmother when she was a young woman.

The song was an old love song, and as Miles sang it under his breath, his eyes held a far-away look, wistful and sad. There was nothing wrong with his memory at the moment, Danny could tell. The light in his eyes was sharp and clear as he reminisced about the woman he had lost to illness years before Danny had come to live with him.

It was a sweet moment, if sad, and Danny felt as if he was intruding on it by standing there just outside the door, even if his grandfather was unaware of his presence. He started to close the door, but before he did, he saw Miles lie back on the bed and clasp the picture to his chest.

His song continued, and the corners of his aged mouth turned up in a smile.

It was that smile that Danny thought about as he turned to go back the way he had come.

*

The flight had been easy to book the following morning. Callie had a small bag packed and the address her mother had given to her, but little else.

The stewardess was saying something about emergency exits, but Callie had tuned her and everything else out as she stared unseeingly out of the window of the plane. The plane's engines were rumbling to life in preparation for takeoff. In a matter of hours, she would touch down in Chicago and—hopefully—find her father.

But it was Danny she thought of the entire way there.

CHAPTER TEN

The cab let Callie out in front of an apartment complex that had seen better days. She got warily out of the car and stared up at the second floor. Somehow, she had not pictured her father living in a place as ordinary as this one, or as washed out. She had expected to find him somewhere full of life and color.

But it was just a place in which to lay one's head, she reminded herself. She had spent time in more than one dive herself because it was cheap and available on short notice. What mattered more was how and where you spent your waking hours.

Rather than go in right away, Callie stood as if frozen, still looking up at the second floor. She had been waiting for this day for so long that she was a little embarrassed by her hesitation now. Her mother had warned her that her father might not be glad to see her, but surely there would be some part of him that was. Wouldn't there?

Despite her mother's advice, she found herself wishing now that she had called first.

Finally, she got her feet moving again. They carried her up the front steps and to the elevator. She rode it up to the second floor, and the doors opened to reveal a hall that was just as shabby and drab as everything else in this place. Pulling out the slip of paper with her father's address on it, Callie glanced at it again even though she had already memorized it. She scanned the numbers painted on the doors, some peeling and hard to read, until she found the one she wanted.

Apartment 208.

There was a peephole in it, and she was tempted to press her eye to it and see if she could catch a glimpse of what lay on the other side. Stupid, she thought. Just knock and you'll see well enough when he opens the door. But she hesitated a few moments longer before finally raising her hand—she was surprised to realize the palm was sweaty—and knocking forcefully.

There was no response right away. Maybe her timing was bad, and he was out. She checked her watch. It was mid-afternoon. He might be at work somewhere. She hadn't thought of that when she had taken the cab over here.

But a moment later she heard the sound of footsteps on the other side of the door. Realizing that she was holding her breath, she let it out just as the door opened.

"Yes?"

There was the faintest stirring of recognition in her as she stared at the man before her, but only barely. He had changed. He was not as tall as she remembered, although maybe that was because she had been a very small child the last time she had seen him. The t-shirt and pants he wore had seen better days. His hair was thin and gray, his face half-covered by a salt-and-pepper beard, and he wore glasses now that covered hollow-looking eyes.

He also clearly didn't recognize her. "Yes?" he repeated impatiently, squinting at her with a blank look. "What do you want?"

Her mouth was suddenly dry, but she managed to get one word out. "Dad?"

"I think there must be a mistake, miss," he said, frowning with thinly veiled irritation. "You have the wrong apartment."

"Are you James Sorenson?"

"Yes, but—" He stopped abruptly, and his mouth fell open. "Callie?" he asked finally, his face draining of what little color it had.

She nodded, all of the words she had rehearsed on the way over here abandoning her.

"What . . . what are you doing here?"

It was not exactly a heartwarming welcome, but she hadn't really been naïve enough to expect one. Hoped, maybe, but not expected. She felt a stab of disappointment. "Nice to see you, too, Dad."

At least he had the grace to look embarrassed. He shuffled from one foot to the other, like a child caught in the act. "I . . ."

"I know this is a bit out of the blue, but I've come a long way to see you. Can I come in?"

"Uh, yeah. Of course." Standing to one side, he opened the door a little wider to let her enter. She thought she saw his hand tremble slightly on the door handle.

The apartment had a disheveled look about it with a few half-opened boxes here and some shirts tossed over there. A stack of unopened mail sat in the middle of the floor, and a few pieces had toppled off and scattered onto the carpet. As Callie watched, her father swept them aside with his foot and hastily began removing a pile of books from an armchair so there would be room for her to sit. The furniture she could see was several years out of date and had most likely come with the apartment.

A few framed photographs hung on the wall, the only personal touches in the tiny room. Callie stopped to examine them. Each one showed her father in a different place and with a different group of people. In the nearest one, her father and three other strangers, all heavily tanned, stood on a tropical beach somewhere with their arms around each other and their glasses hoisted aloft in a merry toast. "Jamaica?" she guessed conversationally, trying to cover up the mass of emotions swirling inside her.

There were no pictures of her or Elliot that she could see. Had they not been important enough to him to remember?

"Fiji," her dad corrected, adjusting his glasses. "Please. Sit down."

Turning away from the picture, she sat in the plain but

serviceable armchair, poised on the front half of it instead of settling back into it. Having made it this far, part of her wanted to bolt out the door again.

"Can I get you something to drink? Soda? Beer?"

"No. Thank you."

He sat across her from her on a flowered sofa, clearing his throat and clasping and unclasping his hands nervously.

It was surreal, Callie thought, sitting here at last with the man for whom she had been searching so long, and discussing beverage choices with him. There was really only one thing she wanted to ask him, but somehow it didn't seem appropriate to open with *Why did you walk out on us?*

"So, how are you?" he asked her finally, breaking the uncomfortable silence. "You look well. All grown up, too."

"I'm all right." Emotionally stunted and struggling with commitment issues, she thought, but otherwise just fine.

"And your mom? How's Liddy?"

"Recovering from a broken hip at the moment. But she's doing okay."

"What happened?"

"Fell off a ladder."

She thought he might ask for more details, but he didn't. There was another long, awkward pause. "Let's see . . . you must be, what, in college now?"

He didn't even remember how old she was, Callie realized with an inner pang. "No. I never went to college. I've been traveling around a lot instead. Working. Writing." She hoped he might be curious about her writing and ask questions, or even wonder about where she had traveled. They had that much in common, didn't they? But although his expression remained polite, there was no real flicker of interest in his eyes.

"Ah. The school of life. There's a lot to be said for that form of education, too."

"So I keep telling people." Maybe he would be more interested in sharing what was going on in his life. "What about you? What do you do now?" She couldn't even really remember what he had done before.

"Oh, a little of this, a little of that. I travel around a lot, too. I'll actually be leaving Chicago in a few weeks. Got a thing lined up in Quebec."

"Quebec, huh?" She clasped her hands together much as he had done and stared at them. In another minute, she was likely to ask about the weather. She had not flown halfway across the United States to engage in idle chitchat with the man who had abandoned her as a child, but it was difficult to figure out how to transition to the real topic she wanted to discuss. Her father inadvertently came to her rescue.

"So what brings you to Chicago, Callie?"

He had asked the question pleasantly enough, but Callie stiffened. To see *him*, obviously. Could he really not have guessed that? "You . . . you have to ask?"

He frowned, looking confused.

"I wanted to meet my father," she said bluntly. "Ask a few questions. See how you were doing." She forced herself to look him in the eye. "Find out why you left."

Her bluntness clearly caught him off guard. "I see," he said, trying to suppress a wince as he looked away.

"Do you? I've waited nearly twenty years for some answers. Mom wouldn't give me any." Her voice shook. "What happened, Dad? One day you were there, and then the next day you weren't. Why did you leave?"

A sad smile flickered across his face. "Some people just aren't meant to be tied down. I tried my hand at domestic life, Callie. I just couldn't do it."

"Why not?"

He hesitated, his discomfort growing.

"Tell me," she demanded, hating the fact that her eyes were growing wet. She blinked hard. "I'm a big girl. I can handle it. Was it us? Were we that awful to live with?"

"No, of course not." He ran his fingers through his thin, gray hair. "Look, did you talk with your mother about any of this?"

"I tried. She didn't think it was a good idea."

He muttered something under his breath that sounded like agreement.

Callie leaned forward. "What?"

"I tried explaining it to your mother years ago, but I don't think Liddy ever really understood. There was nothing wrong with you kids, or with her, all right? It was . . . that way of life, the endless sameness of it all that I couldn't take. I was suffocating. You get one shot, kid. One life. One chance to find your happiness. I had to take it."

It felt like someone had kicked her in the stomach. He thought they had been obstacles to his happiness? "And did you find it?"

"Sure," he said, a little too brightly. "Sure. I found the open road. I found freedom."

Freedom from what? she wondered. Besides his wife and children, of course. "I don't understand. What were we to you, some sort of experiment that ended badly?"

"Now, that's not fair—"

"Life's not fair. I learned that lesson at a very young age, thanks to you." She shook her head with a bitter little laugh. "So that's it, then, huh? You left your wife and children to follow your bliss?" She waved an arm at the barren room. "Is this your bliss, Dad? Really?"

He was silent.

"Didn't you ever miss us, or think of us? Didn't we mean anything to you?"

"Of course you did."

"We just didn't mean enough," she finished for him. She had not intended to let her emotions get the best of her, but she had not expected to feel so rejected, either. "Do you have any idea how much time I wasted agonizing over what I must have done to make you go away? And then I blamed Mom. Man, do I owe her a huge apology over that."

"When I left, it wasn't my intention to hurt you."

"Well, that makes it all better, doesn't it?"

"Callie . . ."

She bit her lip to keep from saying more angry words. They would serve no purpose beyond venting. There was one more question she needed answered, but she waited until she felt calmer before speaking again. "Do you know that Elliot's dead?"

Pressing his lips together in a tight line, her father nodded.

If he had struck her, it would have hurt less. Had he merely read about it in some newspaper, detached and distant, or had her mother somehow contacted him and then kept that secret, too? "Why didn't you come to his funeral?"

"I sent flowers."

"You sent flowers," she repeated.

"That part of my life was over, Callie. I had closed the door on it a long time ago. What would have been the point in going there then?"

"Oh, I don't know . . . mourning your dead son?"

"I mourned for Elliot in my own way. I don't expect you to understand."

"Good, because I don't."

Her father sat tight-lipped again. Watching him, Callie thought she understood now why her mother had thought it best not to tell her children much about him. It was a hurtful thing for a child to realize her father had never really loved her except maybe in a mild, disinterested sort of way, whether she was four years old or twenty-four.

And to think she had used to believe there was some deep meaning behind her father's choice to abandon them. It made her feel sick to think about how much of her life she had wasted trying to understand her father, maybe even trying to emulate him. He was not at all the man she had imagined he might be. She had often pictured him as a Jack Kerouac sort of figure, searching for hidden truths behind every day experiences, and driven by that search to leave his home and family. She used to like to think that maybe that restlessness was something they had in common, but now . . .

Flowers, she thought to herself in numb disbelief. At least when Liddy had awakened in the hospital after surgery it was to find Callie there with her, not just an arrangement of flowers. Maybe she was less like her father than she had thought.

The man before her now struck her as a washed-out version of what she had expected. He was searching less for truth and more for a good time. And from what she could see, he was still searching. The only thing they had in common was DNA.

"What do you want from me, an apology? I'm sorry. I'm sorry you kids and Liddy were hurt by my leaving, but I had to do what I thought was best. To stay would have meant living a lie, because it would have meant denying who I really was."

"No," Callie said, shaking her head. "I don't need an apology from you. I just needed to know why." Swallowing hard, she stood up from the chair. "I think it's time for me to go."

There was undisguised relief on her father's face. This had not been a happy reunion for either of them. "If you think that's best," he said politely, rising from his seat, too. He followed her to the door.

Once there, she stopped and turned back to him. "I didn't come here looking for a fight. Really, I didn't." Her anger slowly dissipated, replaced by a deflated feeling. She felt like she was four years old again and fruitlessly waiting for her father to come home and scoop her up in his arms again. It was never going to happen. "I just—I wanted to see my father."

"The thing is, Callie—I really think it would be better if we don't do this again. I'm sorry."

So was she, but she only nodded.

There was no goodbye hug at the door, or even so much as a handshake. Neither of them was sorry that she was leaving. She took one last long look at him, trying and failing to find the slightest hint of the man she thought she remembered. He looked faded somehow. Washed out and empty.

And worried, she realized with some surprise. Her presence here, however brief, had disrupted the life he had created for himself, and he was anxious for it to return to the way it was. For a man who claimed to have run away from the endless sameness of family life, she wondered if he could see that his rootlessness had a bleak sameness all its own. She glanced back into his apartment, shabby and bare of most personal touches, and she suspected it was just one in a long string of similar places. It seemed so sad to her that, hurt as she was, she couldn't summon any more anger toward him. "Goodbye, Dad. I hope you find what you're looking for."

"Goodbye, Callie."

The door closed behind her as she left, and she walked away without a backward glance, thinking numbly that it was highly unlikely that she would ever see him again. She was just a chapter in his life, and one that he was done with. He had been for a long time. It was time for her to be finished with it, too.

The day in the park that she remembered spending with her father so many years ago came back to her then. She started to cry and earned a startled look from a tenant she passed on her way back to the elevator. But it was a cathartic release of long pent-up emotions, and she felt lighter somehow when she was done, if exhausted. The man for whom she had been searching for so long didn't exist anymore, so she could finally stop trying to find him.

I hope you find what you're looking for. Those had been Danny's last words to her before she left.

Out on the street, she hailed a cab. She had had enough of searching. Enough traveling around. She was tired.

She wanted to go home.

CHAPTER ELEVEN

The back-to-back red-eyes along with the meeting with her father left Callie feeling exhausted. She fumbled wearily with her keys at her mother's front door for a long time before realizing that she was trying to use the wrong key to unlock the door. While she was still trying to find the right key, the door opened to reveal Liddy's surprised face.

"Callie? I thought maybe it was just a burglar who was lousy at his job. When did you get back?"

"About an hour ago."

"Did you find him?"

Callie nodded without much energy.

Her mom opened the door wider. "Come inside."

Callie stepped past her mother and let her bag drop on the floor beside the door before allowing herself to collapse on the couch.

Liddy sat down beside her. "So. Are you all right?"

"Not yet, but I'll get there. It went pretty much the way you thought it would."

"I'm sorry, honey."

"Don't be. If anything, I owe you an apology. You just wanted to protect me from the fact that my father never really wanted me."

Her mother put an arm around her. "I think he loved us as much as he could love anything. He just didn't have the stamina for marriage or parenthood. It ain't for wimps."

Callie smiled a humorless smile. "I think you might be giving him too much credit, but I appreciate the effort to make me feel better."

"Do you regret going to see him?"

"No. I had to go." She blinked rapidly, surprised that she still had a few tears left in her after all. "It did hurt, though. I thought he'd at least be a little glad to see me."

"I'm sorry. I wish it could have been different."

"I really thought that maybe if I figured out what it was he left us to go looking for, everything would just kind of make sense, you know? Suddenly my whole life would fall into place. But I don't think *he* even really knows. I could be wrong, of course—"

"I don't think you are," Liddy said softly.

"At any rate, I don't think he's got the answers to life that I thought he had. He did open my eyes to one thing, though."

"Which was?"

"I don't want to follow in his footsteps."

Her mother seemed to hold her breath. "No?"

"It's just so . . . I don't know." She shrugged wearily. "It's like it doesn't mean anything."

"What doesn't?"

"His life. It's not *about* anything. Or anyone. There's just nothing there."

"Sounds very lonely."

Liddy's voice was sad, and Callie looked at her, wondering if there was still a part of her that loved her father. She reached for her mother's hand. "You never told me that he knew about Elliot's death and chose not to come to the funeral."

"No. That was one piece of information I had planned to keep to myself."

There was a lot that her mother had carried alone that Callie had never realized before. "I'm sorry, Mom."

"For what?"

"For never really understanding before how hard it must have been for you when Dad left. Then Elliot on top of that. Then me leaving . . ."

"Baby girl, life's been hard sometimes, but *you* have always been my joy, never my burden. Don't ever think otherwise."

"I think you're an amazing woman, Mom. More so than I ever realized. And I hope you know that I love you."

"I love you, too." Her mother hugged her and then wiped at her eyes. "Good Lord, Callie. The past few days have been filled with more soul baring than a year's worth of therapy. Think of all the money we've saved in psychiatry bills."

They smiled tentatively at each other, and Callie felt as if for the first time in a long time, she had really come home again. "I'm sure we're both still crazy enough to benefit from a little professional help," she returned, her voice not as steady as usual.

"Most likely, yes. But a little 'crazy' keeps life interesting." The expression on Liddy's face grew more serious. "So, what now, Callie? Where do you plan to go from here?"

She looked down at her hands. Putting down roots might still be beyond her, but if there was one place where she could do it, it would be here, with Liddy. With Danny. "I've been on the road an awful lot. I think I'd like to stay put for a little while. See if I can explore the world a little closer to home."

"I think that sounds like a very good idea."

"Don't get me wrong," Callie said quickly, glancing up again. "I may not be Dad, but I still may want to see someplace new from time to time. That's just part of who I am, and I don't think there's anything wrong with that."

"No, of course not. But you're very welcome to stay here as long as you want. Any time you want." Her voice softened. "And Danny? What about him?"

"I'll answer that question just as soon as I figure it out."

*

Danny glanced at the clock on the wall above the brochures. Not yet ten o'clock. Em would be in soon to cover the phone.

Now that his mind was made up, he was impatient. Impatient to get everything finalized, impatient to get out of here and go where he needed to be. See who he needed to see. He still had a couple of calls to make and cancellations to explain, but he thought he would have everything covered by noon. His grandfather, the business, and anything else that might need attention while he was away. He would call Liddy next. He wondered if she had heard from Callie yet.

Callie. He couldn't think of her without thinking of the way she had looked at him on his grandfather's porch. There was nothing casual about that look. He knew it even if she didn't.

He reached for the phone, intending to call Liddy, when the door opened. He looked up, expecting to see Em.

Instead, he saw Callie.

*

"Hi." She was going to have to start thinking of something better than that to say each time she saw him.

He stared at her, clearly shocked to see her, and slowly put down the phone receiver he had been holding. "Hi."

She cleared her throat and took a step forward. "Is this a bad time?"

"Uh . . . no. Not at all." Danny looked completely bewildered. Callie would have preferred to see a warmer emotion on his face, but she supposed it was what she deserved. "But I thought you were in Chicago."

"I was. Short trip."

"Oh."

He had not moved from behind the desk, and Callie's nerves took a hit. Was he at all happy to see her, or not? She couldn't tell.

He was either still in shock or wary. She couldn't blame him in either case.

She edged forward. "So, I found my dad."

"And?" he asked quietly.

"Well . . ." She smiled without mirth. "Turns out he's even more screwed up than I am. He lives alone, floats from place to place, and tries to figure out just what it is he wants out of life. I don't think he's any closer to finding it than he was when he left us. But he made it very clear that it doesn't include anything to do with me."

"I'm sorry."

"But it was good I went to see him. It made me realize something."

Finally, he came out from behind the desk, albeit slowly. He leaned back against it with his arms folded across his chest. "And what was that?"

Would he believe her after all of her uncertainty? She hoped he could hear the sincerity in her voice. "That I'm not my father. He wanted to cut ties with the people who should have been the most important ones in his life. I don't want to make that same mistake."

Danny didn't move a muscle but stood tense and still, as if he was afraid to startle her away with any movement. "What *do* you want to do?"

What she wanted to do was throw her arms around him and kiss him hard, but she didn't feel as if she had a right to do that. Callie took a deep breath. "I want—"

The door opened again, and Em breezed in, breathless. "Okay, I'm here, I'm here. The traffic on the highway today was—" She broke off as she saw the two of them standing there. "Uh . . . am I interrupting something?"

Danny was silent, and Callie faltered in her words.

Em glanced at her watch. "Oh, whoa. Look at that. Ten-oh-two. I'll just go ahead and take my lunch break. Excuse me."

And she hastily retreated the way she had come, closing the door behind her.

Danny still said nothing but only watched Callie.

Callie tried again, hoping he would understand what she was trying to say. "Look, I used to think that the only way I could learn enough about life and the real world to be able to write about it was to leave home, but I think my father and I both made the same mistake in thinking that the real world is 'out there' somewhere. It is, but it's here, too. I guess I was a little narrow-minded with my world view."

"Is that what you came back here to tell me?"

"No, not completely." She took another step toward him. "I'm sorry, Danny."

"Sorry for what? Kissing me?"

Sorry I stopped is more like it, she thought wistfully. "No. I'm sorry if I hurt you the other night when I said I had to figure things out. I didn't mean that I had to figure out my feelings for you. I don't have any doubt about those."

He started to speak, but she quickly raised a hand to stop him, afraid that if she didn't get it out now she might never find the nerve again.

"Just let me get this out first, please. It's been years since my father left my mother, and it's still hard for her to talk about it. He hurt her badly, and I didn't want to risk hurting you like that. You're the last person I'd ever want to do that to, Danny. Please believe me. And I was afraid that I might, because I was afraid I might be a chip off the old block in that department. So I had to go see him. I had to know why we weren't enough to make him happy."

He appeared to hold his breath. "And what did you find out?"

"That he was scared life might pass him by. That he thought we might get in the way of something better."

"I'm sorry, Callie."

"Well . . ." She shrugged, trying not to let her hurt feelings show. "It sure wasn't the reason I was expecting, but at least now I know."

"And now that you know?"

"I want to make sure life doesn't pass me by, either." For better or for worse, it was time to make her pitch. "So I came here to collect on that favor."

He furrowed his brow, bewildered again. "What favor?"

"Ah, you trying to get out of the bet after all?" she asked, trying to keep her tone light but hearing the unsteadiness in her voice. "Our pool game. Remember?"

The confusion in his eyes cleared, and he nodded slowly.

"So I'm here to call it in."

"What do you want?"

"I want you to, well . . . consider, at least—" She was losing her courage and botching this up. Wasn't she supposed to be good with words? But somehow she didn't think she'd ever had as much riding on the right words as she did now. What if he decided she was too fickle for him to take a chance on her?

At least he was still listening. "Consider . . . ?"

"Me?" she finished lamely.

"Consider you," he repeated.

She nodded, and when she spoke again there was a catch in her voice. "I don't blame you if you if you have doubts about me, but I really think we could—"

"Callie?"

"Yes?" she trailed off, fearing the worst.

He stared at her for a moment, and then he gave a self-deprecating laugh that did remarkable things to her insides and shook his head. "Do you know what I was doing when you walked in just now?"

"No," she said, startled by the change in topic.

"I was in the middle of clearing the books for the next few days and making arrangements to close up for a little while."

"Why?" She was suddenly worried, thinking there was only one reason why he would do that, and it wasn't good. "Oh, Danny . . . Did something happen with your grandfather?"

"No. Well, nothing like what you mean," he corrected. "It's more like what happened to me, watching him. His life has not been easy, you know that? He's had a long, hard road already and it looks like there's more of the same ahead. But he hangs on to the good stuff. I don't know how much time he and I will have left together, but I want to make the most of the good stuff with him."

"I see," she said, still a little confused by where he was going with this.

"What happened between you and me the other day, that's the good stuff, too, Callie." Danny pushed himself up from the desk. "I was watching my grandfather and realizing that life's too short not to take a few chances. So I thought it would be worth the risk to track you down and try to convince you that maybe we shouldn't play it safe. Now, for all I knew, you might tell me I'm nuts and to get the message already, but—"

"No, no, no," she said hastily, a wonderfully warm feeling filling her as her hopes rose. "I wouldn't do that."

A slow smile spread across his beautiful face. "So I was just about to call your mom and try to find out if you were still in Chicago or heading to New York, or God knows where else. And Em was good enough to agree to come in today on short notice and cover the desk so I could go home and pack a bag."

"I always liked Em."

"Me too."

Her heart started beating faster. "So you're not—upset or anything? Angry?"

"It was hard to watch you drive away. Very hard. I don't think I'd handle it well if you decided to do it again."

"I'm not going to do it again."

"Point is, Callie, if you're asking me to 'consider you,' I'm already on board. When all is said and done, I'd rather take a chance with you than without you."

She let out a shaky breath and felt an almost irresistible urge to weep with relief. "Oh. Well, that makes things a lot simpler, then."

Then she crossed the floor and threw herself into his arms so hard that he staggered back against the desk again, taking him with her.

He started to laugh, no easy feat when she had nearly knocked the wind out of him. "Try not to put me in the hospital, okay?"

"Sorry." She pulled back enough to look him in the face. "I'd take good care of you, though. I have a wonderful bedside manner."

"I'll just bet you do." Still grinning, Danny framed her face between his hands and bent his head to kiss her tenderly.

This time there were no conflicting feelings, no doubts about whether or not she should do this. Callie wrapped her fingers in his hair and gave herself up entirely, reveling in the feel of him in her arms. Her breath caught in her throat when she thought how close she had come to missing out on this, missing out on him.

He heard the catch of her breath and drew back. "Are you okay?"

She nodded, struggling to speak. "Just happy," she managed finally, smiling up at him through eyes that had grown wet again. She was turning into quite the emotional mess lately.

"Good. I like you happy."

"I'm still pretty screwed up, you know."

"Yeah?" He kissed her again, his lips trailing from her mouth to her throat in a way that left her lightheaded.

"And I still may want to hit the road from time to time," she continued breathlessly, wanting to be completely honest with him but finding it harder and harder to form coherent thoughts. "That part hasn't changed. But I'll always come back, Danny. Always."

His arms around her tightened as if he would never let her go, and she sighed and tilted her head so he could trace the length of her neck with his lips.

Danny McCutcheon had very strong lips.

His breath came out warm against her skin. "Maybe I'll go with you from time to time."

"I think I would like that." Callie guided his mouth up to hers again and kissed him until he had to catch his own breath.

"Careful," he warned her, his eyes never leaving her mouth. "We don't want to shock Em if she walks in here again."

"All right. Then let's get out of here so she can start her shift already, and we can go someplace where we won't shock anybody."

Danny smiled a slow smile at her and put his arm around her waist as she pulled him toward the door. "Welcome home, Callie."

EPILOGUE

The following summer

The sun was hot overhead. Before much longer, Callie would have to take another quick dip in the water to cool off again. But she was reluctant to move just yet, stretched out on the picnic blanket with Danny's arms around her as she was. They had just finished eating lunch in their secluded little beach, "their" spot, and she felt lazy and content.

They had come here today with no other reason other than just to enjoy it together, but Callie decided it was as good a time and place as any to share her news with him.

"You know that editor I've been exchanging emails with?" she asked nonchalantly, idly stroking Danny's bronzed arm with her fingers.

"Mm, hmm."

"Well, he liked my book idea. The one with the collection of essays? He wants to see what I've got so far."

Danny rolled her over so he could look her in the eyes. "Congratulations." He kissed her once, briefly, then again, long and leisurely. "I know how hard you've been working on that. You must be thrilled."

She shrugged but allowed herself a smile. "Yeah, a little. Nothing's written in stone yet, but it could happen."

"We should celebrate. Care for another apple juice on the rocks?"

"Oooh, you're breaking out the good stuff. This must be a big deal."

"Don't move. I'll be right back."

Callie stretched languidly and closed her eyes. It still seemed somewhat amazing to her that she could be so happy. This was not exactly the script she had thought her life would follow. Thank heavens for rewrites, she thought with an inward smile.

She heard rustling sounds as the man she loved rummaged through their cooler. A minute later he was back beside her on the blanket, propped up on one elbow and handing her a cold drink.

She sat up to take it from him before turning her eyes to the serene pool of water glistening with sunlight on its surface. "Thanks. Perfect day, isn't?"

"Beautiful." After a moment, Danny cleared his throat. "Callie . . ."

"Yes?" She glanced over at him and saw him holding out a folded piece of paper to her. "What's that?"

"I may not be the writer here, but I did put a lot of thought into this."

Curious, she unfolded the note and read it. It had only two words but there was a golden ring taped right beneath them.

Marry me.

She blinked. "I—" Once upon a time she would have expected such words to fill her with panic and send her running. There was nothing like that now, only a thrilling sort of shiver down her spine and a feeling that everything was exactly as it should be now.

"Yeah . . . ?"

"I . . . I think you're a very good writer," she said finally in a voice that had gone all husky on her.

He kissed her shoulder, and then her lips. "I love you, Callie. In my whole life, you are the best chance I have ever taken."

Her voice grew even thicker. "I love you, too."

"So is that a yes?"

"Oh—yes," she agreed with a slow-spreading smile. "Yes, it is."

He took the ring from off of the note, and Callie held her left hand out to him. The ring slid on smoothly, and its single diamond sparkled in the sunlight.

Danny wrapped his hand around hers. "What do you think?"

"I think my mom is going to give me the biggest 'I told you so' in recorded history—" Callie smiled at him, "—when I tell her I'm going to marry Danny McCutcheon."

ABOUT THE AUTHOR

Christine S. Feldman writes both novels and feature-length screenplays, and she has placed in screenwriting competitions on both coasts. She lives in the Pacific Northwest with her ballroom-dancing husband and their beagle.

A SNEAK PEEK FROM CRIMSON ROMANCE

From *Unattainable* by Leslie P. Garcia
http://www.crimsonromance.com/upcoming-releases-romance-ebook/
unattainable

CHAPTER ONE

Jovani Treviño slipped from the pickup, his boots thudding dully on the dry soil as he looked around carefully but not with particular unease. A crescent moon climbed up over the far side of the interstate, but here darkness allowed considerable isolation. Cars speeding by on the freeway wouldn't notice him, and if they did, hopefully they'd avert their eyes, assuming someone needed to take a leak.

Only moments passed before a second, dark vehicle pulled in behind him. The driver switched off the headlights but left the parking lights on. Jovi reached into the cab and pulled the lever to open the hood then moved to the front of the truck. Seconds later the newcomer joined him, extending his hand briefly.

"Jovi."

"Hey, Rick." Almost immediately, both turned their attention to the engine.

"So—you gonna apply for the job at *Nueva Brisa?*" the newcomer asked.

"Tomorrow," Jovi agreed, turning at a slight rustle in the weeds that framed the roadside clearing, then relaxing when he realized the noise couldn't have come from anything large.

"Still jumping at shadows?" Rick shook his head. "We leave the job, but the edge never leaves."

"You don't let anyone leave," Jovi retorted, slapping a mosquito seconds too late, and rubbing his arm. "Tell me why I said yes again."

"Cause you're one of the good guys, we pay well, and you get to be close to your mom while she gets back on her feet. It's win-win, Jovi."

"Cut the bull, friend. I left DEA because no one wins—the work's important, but the war's unwinnable, Rick."

Rick Ortega shrugged his thin shoulders. "Maybe."

"And this one smells."

"Why?" He nudged Jovi with an elbow. "Cause we're looking at some honey the locals call untouchable?"

"Unattainable." Jovi motioned Ortega back and slammed the hood. "Your reasons for looking at this woman are shaky at best, and if I'm investigating her, I damn sure won't be thinking about her looks."

"Touchier than ever," the DEA agent muttered.

"And in a week or two, when my plane lands in Florida—I'm done, Rick. No more arm-twisting, no favors. I'm serious."

"Look, I know you mostly came until your mom beats her pneumonia—not so much to help us. But you're perfect, Jovi—the border's home to you, but you've been gone long enough you're an outsider now."

"Hell, I was always an outsider. Everywhere."

"Whining isn't your style, *amigo*," Ortega chided. "You know how things are. No trust left—our side or theirs. The cartels are winning. For Christ's sake, they're slaughtering innocents on the streets a mile from here." He jerked his head toward the tree-framed skyline. Behind those trees, the Rio Grande whispered its newly violent song to the night. "Check her out, that's all. She worked for a major importer, but quit suddenly. Her father left her some money, but—" He shook his head. "Something's not right, buddy."

Jovi glanced at him. "Because her father left money?"

"No. Because insurance aside, her father shouldn't have had money to leave. The ranch is a joke—big property value, but no livestock except horses. On paper, he sold horses—horses we're not real sure existed. Horses! No market for horses right now, going on back even before his death. The man went through a bitter divorce from the wife, yet got big bucks from the ex father-in-law, Lionel De Cordova."

"De Cordova? Man!" The name surprised him. "But for all his sins, I never heard he trafficked."

"We know some of the younger cousins do. Nobody's tagged him, true. But the foreman you're replacing? Arrested in Sinaloa several weeks ago. Arranging to drive a load to El Paso."

"So she has to know?"

Ortega shrugged. "Hard to say. The man's a Mexican national, and the story wasn't broadcast here. We only found out through our sources. But if he worked out of her barn . . ."

"She either knows or she's stupid?" he suggested.

Again, Ortega made a slight gesture of denial. "She'd been in New York and Houston more than home until recently. She worked for an import firm with headquarters in Houston and branches all over Mexico, as well as in several border towns. The horses were more or less at the mercy of the foreman and the two grooms."

"Sketchy at best," Jovi pointed out again. "This is my last call, though," he repeated, walking to the driver's side and pulling the door open. "This job's too hard on the soul, Rick. Too much lying and too many half-truths—and to save what? "

Ortega paused by the open door as his friend climbed back in. "Did I tell you that little four-year old girl—Lisa, remember her? She turned seven yesterday. They put her photo on one of those news lead-ins."

"Damn you," Jovi snarled, thinking of the child he, Ortega, and others had found cowering in the corner of a crack house after a deal turned particularly violent. And her brothers, 5 and 8, lying broken on the floor in their own blood. His last official case—the last case he'd tried to stomach.

"Sometimes we win," Rick insisted, and slapped his arm. "*Suerte*," he ended, walking away.

Luck. Jovi shook his head, turned on the truck, and poked the radio button. He wouldn't need luck if he kept his mind on work and on the stable full of thoroughbreds waiting for him in Florida. As he eased back onto the access road, blessed darkness and George Strait's melodious voice surrounded him.

In the mood for more Crimson Romance? Check out *On the Fly* by Katie Kenyhercz at CrimsonRomance.com.